MINETOWN MURDER

"Where were you, McCoy?" Jessica screamed. "You could have stopped those killers. They marched Shorty Clawson through town and then stoned him to death."

"That harmless drunk I talked to yesterday? He couldn't hurt a fly."

"They said he talked too much about what happened here before. This was another warning to the people of Timber Break not to talk to strangers."

McCoy slammed his hand against the wall. "I was set up. Cheyenne Barton was giving me a tour of the river area. They wanted me out of town and they arranged it."

McCoy marched down the street to the big three-story mansion where Cheyenne Barton lived. He went to the front door and stomped inside.

"Cheyenne, where the hell are you? You murdering bitch. You and your friends are all going to pay for this!"

Also in the *Spur* Series from *Leisure Books:*

SPUR

MINETOWN MISTRESS

DIRK FLETCHER

LEISURE BOOKS   **NEW YORK CITY**

A LEISURE BOOK®

June 1993

Published by

Dorchester Publishing Co., Inc.
276 Fifth Avenue
New York, NY 10001

Copyright © 1993 by Chet Cunningham/BookCrafters

Printed in the United States of America.

Chapter One

The sound of the rifle shot and the splintering rush of hot lead through the thin side of the old Concord stage came almost at the same instant and sent Spur McCoy ducking to the floor. He grabbed his Spencer repeating rifle, loaded with eight rounds of .52 caliber bullets.

McCoy leaned to the edge of the window and saw only two men riding hard from the rear, one at an angle to cut them off. He pushed the rifle barrel across the woman's lap to his right and aimed out the flapping canvas of the window.

He sighted in on the head of the charging horse 40 yards away and fired. The heavy slug and the horse met on a perfect collision course. The roan took the bullet just behind her left eye, her front legs collapsing, and the rider went off the saddle over the mount's head as she rolled into the green grass of the Idaho mountain meadow.

The attacker on the other side was closing in with a carbine. Spur shifted the rifle out of the other window, found his target and immediately fired twice since the holdup man had his weapon up and ready to fire.

The robber's finger never pulled the trigger. The .52 caliber slug caught him just below his collar bone, slammed him off the mount and sent him rolling down a slight bank on the far side of the road.

The woman had put her hands over her ears when the first round came through the sideboards. Now she lowered them.

"Two down and out, nice shooting." Her voice was pleasantly low, and she smiled as she looked at Spur.

He glanced at her. She was young, maybe 22, with a pert nose, a pretty face and a traveling dress that covered up everything below her chin so a man could only guess and hope what was hidden from view. He bet she was no pig in a poke.

"Thank you, Miss. I hate being shot at." The two men across the way nodded.

"Good shooting," the shorter one said. "I couldn't get my weapon out of my pocket. Then again it's only a derringer, not good for more than about six feet."

The other man smiled and nodded. He was older, wore a black suit and a black low-crowned town hat.

The stage slowed down, and when it came to a stop, the driver dropped down to the side and opened the door.

"Everyone all right in there?" he asked.

"Fine, thanks to this gentleman," the woman said. "He picked off both of them like it was something he did all the time."

The driver eyed McCoy a minute, then grinned. "Mighty obliged. This here ride's on the company. Policy. Anybody helps out on an attempted holdup rides free. Take care of it at the end of your trip. Where you headed?"

"Timber Break."

"See you there."

The driver returned to his seat and the rig moved away shortly. The short man who was a drummer looked at McCoy. "You really getting off at Timber Break? It's not much of a town."

"I've never been there."

"Take it from me, don't stay long. I represent Connecticut Cutlery and have to stop and service three stores. Not much business, but it's on my route. I get out the next day. It's one damn weird town. They treat strangers there like they have the pox. Damn peculiar. Oh, pardon my language, Miss."

She smiled. "I've heard worse. I'm stopping at Timber Break as well. Why is it a weird town?"

The drummer fidgeted in his seat, looked out the window and glanced at the black-suited man. "Sir, are you from Timber Break?"

The man across from McCoy shook his head. "Boise."

"Good. Anyway Timber Break is a strange little place. People are clannish, unfriendly. Hardly give a stranger the time of day. I'd get in and out quick as my business permitted."

"I'm going there to stay with my aunt," the young

woman said. "She lives there."

McCoy had been well-aware of the pretty girl since they first boarded the coach six hours ago. It was the first time they had spoken. She had fair skin, soft billowing hair the color of ripe strawberries and a perky little nose that made her face a delight. Wide-set green eyes caught him looking at her, and she grinned at him.

"Maybe us newcomers will have to stick together in Timber Break," she said.

McCoy touched the brim of his hat and nodded.

Two hours later they swung down a short slope and into a small valley with a towering line of mountains behind it. The town seemed pasted against the slopes and bordered a chattering stream. Probably 200 people, maybe a few more, Spur estimated as he stepped down from the coach. He reached up to help the girl down.

"My name is Jessica Edwards. I'll be staying with Wilda Edwards. She runs the women's wear store in town."

She said it quickly and softly so no one else could hear, then she went to the boardwalk in front of the stage depot and greeted an older woman.

McCoy collected his one carpetbag, shouldered his Spencer rifle and headed for the walk where the driver caught up with him.

"Sir, I'd like to shake your hand. That pair has been pestering us for a month now. They never got close enough for us to use the shotgun, so you did us a real favor. Manager'll be glad to refund your fare."

McCoy went with the driver into the stage office and looked around. He listened to the account the

driver told of his shooting and then took the $14.53
the manager handed him.

"We're grateful to you sir. I'll need your name to
put on my books as an expense."

"McCoy. Spur McCoy."

"Thank you. I hope you enjoy your stay in Timber
Break."

McCoy didn't move but looked up at the manager.
"Might be a favor you could do for me, sir. I'm
looking for work. You need any hands here in your
stables or harnessing up? Anything at all?"

The manager frowned, then shook his head. "Wish
I did. Might let you ride shotgun, but I'm full. Hired
a new man yesterday, but I think the livery could use
a wrangler. You might try down there. Just a block
down on the right. This isn't a big place, so we don't
have a lot of places to work. The silver mine that
used to support this whole area is closed, which hurts
everybody."

McCoy nodded. "Thank you much, sir. I'll surely
give the livery a try."

McCoy shouldered his Spencer, picked up his
carpetbag and went outside to find the livery. They
did have an opening, mainly because the stage company had offered their stableboy a dollar a week more
than he was making at the livery.

The manager was short and bald, with spectacles
and fringes of white hair around his ears and neck.
He wore a vest over an undershirt and baggy black
pants.

"Five dollars a week, ten hours a day six A.M. to
six P.M., and six days a week."

"I'll take it," McCoy said. He stowed his rifle and

carpetbag in an empty stall next to the big feed box, then grabbed a pitchfork and began cleaning stalls and putting down fresh straw. He grinned at the boss's mathematics. He said ten hours a day, but six to six was twelve. McCoy could stand it for a few days so he could do some quiet investigating.

The owner's name was J.B. Ranger. He looked about 50, a dour, sour, no-nonsense man. Pinched every penny he ever held, Spur guessed. At least Spur had a job in what was reported to be an unfriend- ly town.

Now, all he had to do was find Colonel Amos Potter, learn what his trouble was, help him out of it, and then complete the colonel's mission that the President had sent him here to do. It was so secret that not even General Halleck, Spur's boss in Washington D.C., knew it.

Spur smiled when he remembered Jessica Edwards who had shared the coach with him. He might just have to take her up on her offer of standing together against the unfriendly town. A few days and he'd know a lot more. He had the idea a low profile would be good on this assignment. First he'd find out the temperament of the town and if the sheriff could be trusted.

It looked like one of those tough to impossible cases.

McCoy worked until the sweat stained through his shirt. He took off his vest and hung it near his carpet- bag. Spur McCoy had been a Secret Service Agent for several years now, working directly for General Wilton D. Halleck in Washington. He had as his responsibility the whole western part of the country beyond the Mississippi river.

He had been assigned the west because he was the best shot and best rider in that new group of Special Service Agents. The agency had begun in 1859 with the sole responsibility of protecting the currency. Since that time the agency's tasks had multiplied until now they handled almost any case where the U.S. government was involved or federal laws were violated. They also responded when local jurisdiction pleaded for help from the federal government because they could get no satisfaction from their county, territory or state governments.

Spur McCoy stood two inches over six feet and weighed in at a slender, heavily muscled 180 pounds. He was tanned and fit and had dark hair. On this trip he was clean-shaven except for a dark moustache. He had a cleft in his chin and a thin knife scar on his left cheek that showed up more when he was well-tanned.

McCoy was an expert shot with all types of guns, could use a blacksnake whip, a fighting knife, a staff and his bare hands to subdue an opponent. He knew 20 ways to kill a man if it became necessary to save his own or some civilian's life.

He grew up in New York City where his father had an import business, graduated from Harvard University in Boston, served the U.S. Senator from New York for two years as an aide in Washington, and rose to the rank of captain of infantry during the Civil War. Now he served his country again as a Secret Service Agent.

"Hey, boy!" the boss shouted. "I need that bay with a white splotch on her forehead. Bring her in from the corral and put a saddle on her. Cinch her up tight. That old whore likes to swell up when you put on the cinch strap."

McCoy grinned and found the animal in the corral, dropped a loop of a lasso over her head and brought her into the stable where the boss pointed to a saddle and blanket. One stiff punch to the belly made the bay let out her held-in air, and he cinched the saddle down tight.

Ranger watched a moment, grunted and then led the animal out to the tall man in a black suit who had rented her. When the man had mounted and rode off, Ranger nodded toward him.

"Whenever Mr. Halverson comes in, he'll want that same bay. Thinks he owns her. Could have for the rent he pays on her sometimes three days a week. He's probably the richest man in town, a real force, so whatever you do, don't cross him. Just mind your own business and you'll get along here. We ain't a fussy lot, but we mind our own P's and Q's."

McCoy nodded and went back to cleaning stalls and adding fresh straw.

At six that evening, Spur washed off his boots with water and an old burlap sack, then picked up his carpetbag and went to Main Street. He found Miss Edward's Ladies Wear store two down from the small bank. He looked in the front door and saw Jessica who held up one finger while he waited outside. She came out a moment later.

"Well, I didn't expect to see you so soon."

"I got a job at the livery."

"I'm working in the store. I didn't know she'd want

me to work, but I guess it won't hurt me."

"Jessica, my name is Spur McCoy. Could I buy you some supper?"

"My goodness, no. I don't know you at all. Besides, Aunt Wilda is home fixing something special. I'm about to close."

Spur grinned. "Way it goes. I'll get a hotel room for now, maybe a boarding house later on. I better go."

She touched his shoulder. "I didn't mean to be so abrupt about not having supper with you. I appreciate the offer. I hope you ask me again in a few days." She smiled, turned and hurried into the store.

McCoy had supper at the nearest café, then registered at the town's only hotel, a two story affair, and dropped into bed. He was asleep before he could get his clothes off. He wasn't used to working with a pitchfork for six hours.

The next morning as McCoy ate breakfast at the Ox-Bow Café, he reviewed what he knew about Colonel Potter. The man was 49 years old, retired from the army on a pension and a good friend of General Halleck, Spur's boss in Washington. They had a letter from the colonel postmarked at Longtree, the small town just before Timber Break, so it was certain that Potter got that far.

Timber Break had been his destination. The stage company man at Longtree had said that a man named General Potter had been on board the run one day over two months ago. When he'd caused a ruckus at the depot, the sheriff had come and calmed things down and taken the general's name for a report.

Potter could be calling himself a general now.

Sounded about right. If Spur knew Potter's mission it would make it easy, but Spur was flying blind. He had no papers to identify himself, and no telegram listing his mission. That way it would stay confidential. He wasn't going to start asking questions about Colonel Potter here in town. From what the drummer had said, it was a closed society, an unfriendly bunch.

He'd work at the livery for two days and see what he could find out.

That morning at the livery he talked to four men who rented horses and a man and a woman who took out a buggy. He learned little from any of them. His most innocent question was turned aside or given a one word answer.

Instead of having lunch at noon, Spur went to the stage depot and asked the manager who usually drove in from the south.

"I have twelve different drivers through here. One or two just drive here and turn around. Free to talk to any of them. Still thank you for taking care of that pair of galoots who been pestering us with those robbery attempts. Doubt if we see them again."

Spur talked to three of the drivers. They were playing a penny ante poker game in a big room in back that had six bunks in it for overnight driver accommodations.

"Hunting my cousin who came through here about two months ago. Wonder if any of you seen him?"

"We see dozens of folks," one driver said drawing to a three card straight showing. "Can't remember them all. Fact is, don't remember many of them. He strange or weird or something?"

"Weird, yeah. Thinks he's in the damn army all the time. Thinks he's a general."

"Did have a damn general through a while ago," another driver said. "Hell, I never liked officers. Did a bit in the big war and hated the damn officers."

Spur shrugged. "Crazy Willy. Maybe he thinks he's a general now. About how old was this jasper?"

The driver scowled. "Hell, I'd say he was maybe fifty, ramrod straight. Marched instead of walking. Treated us like we was dirt. I dropped his bag twice just to fix him, but he ignored me like I was trash."

"Hell, don't sound like my cousin. Too old. You kicked this asshole in the crotch, I hope," Spur said.

They all laughed. "Damn well should have," the driver said. "He got off here but I had to go on to Boise. Next time I was through here I asked somebody about the general, but they said he left a couple of days after he arrived."

Spur thanked them, not wanting to push it. These men were not local, so he figured they might be a little easier to talk to. None of it would get back to the locals.

He walked out of the stage office and nearly bumped into Jessica Edwards.

"I waited around for you," Jessica said. "I saw you go in the stage office and wondered if you were leaving town."

Spur smiled. "Hi, good to see you. Not going anywhere. Just talking." She was a fine surprise. Today she wore a close-fitting calico dress with a pinched-in waist that showed her full bosom.

"Is that supper invite still open?" she asked with a sly smile.

"Indeed it is, Miss Edwards. I could pick you up at your shop at six."

"That would be fine, Mr. McCoy. I'll look forward to that. I've decided this is a terrible town. Nobody will say more than two words to me. One woman told me flat out that she doesn't like strangers in her town."

"It is an unusual little place. I can vouch for that. I got to get back to work at the livery. See you at six."

He did the stalls, brushed down two horses, then walked out a mount that came in lathered. It was the bay that the man in the black suit always rode. Nobody said why the bay was foamed up with sweat. The boss just handed the reins to Spur and told him to walk her out of town a mile and then walk her back which he did.

He saddled four more horses, then unsaddled three and rubbed them down. Just before five he put out oats and hay for the mounts in the stalls and some hay for the corral horses.

He washed up, cleaned off his boots, and put on a clean shirt and pants in his hotel room before he met Jessica at her shop. He was ten minutes late, but she had waited for him.

They ate at the best place in town, the Coronet Café. It had checkered tablecloths and a hint at quality, but the food was down home and hearty. They settled for beef stew and cherry pie. He watched amazed as she ate. Her food vanished in half the time his did.

She looked up and grinned. "Sorry, eating fast is a habit I can't get over. When I was younger we had three cousins living with us. If you didn't eat fast you didn't get much to eat."

After the meal it was still light out and he walked her three blocks to her aunt's small brown house. She steered him to the back door, then in one quick move pulled him inside and closed the door.

"Aunt Wilda is at a church meeting tonight," Jessica said. "She said she'd be gone until nine-thirty." Jessica put her arms around him and pulled him against her. She kissed his lips once lightly, then a second time hard and demanding, pressing her breasts tightly against his chest.

When the kiss ended she smiled. "Hope you want to stay a while and get better acquainted."

Spur laughed softly. "Now, Jessie, that's a fine idea." When he bent and kissed her again, this time her lips parted for him.

Chapter Two

Cheyenne Barton never wanted to open her eyes again. If she opened them she would be back in her house. Granted it was an extremely beautiful and well-decorated house, but still it was just a house— not a fantasy wonderland of castles and kings and wonderful beasts and unthinkable beings from other worlds and other planets!

She still felt a billion miles away. Only a slight headache spoiled the serenity of the moment. The headaches always came after one of her fantastic travels into the void of the wondrous unknown. She was euphoric, thankful for her gift of prophecy.

"Missie? Missie, you awake? You back in the land of us alive folks?"

The voice came through to Cheyenne like a roaring of a locomotive or a steamship whistle right in her ear. She threw back the sheet and sat up, her large breasts bouncing and jiggling.

"Gawd dammit, Missie, I figure you was sure enough dead and gone this time."

The speaker was a 13 year-old Chinese girl Cheyenne had picked up for $20 on one of her trips to San Francisco. The girl was curious, outspoken, sassy sometimes and generally a delight.

"Go away, you little bitch!" Cheyenne whispered. "I never want to see your ugly face again."

The girl, Dolly, grinned. "Damnit to fucking hell, Missie, now I knowed you be awake. Got me a message for you. That big fucker from the mine, that long cock Jordan, is in the parlor waiting to see your ass."

"God, child, where did you learn to talk? Jordan? Let me get some clothes on. I have to see him once in a while, otherwise he won't supervise the closed-down mine. I'm still trying to sell it to some demented, rich son-of-a-bitch who wants to own a silver mine."

Cheyenne stretched. She was a half-inch under six feet tall, with solid shoulders from her Russian mother, big breasts, a sleek torso and a flat stomach. She was 32 and had serviced her late husband right into his grave, wearing down his slender pecker until he couldn't get it up anymore. He was 54 at the time, but that was a year ago.

Her slender torso stopped abruptly at her wide hips which quickly slanted down into the most beautiful pair of long legs.

She patted the forest of blonde thatch that hid her crotch. "Hold on, sweetheart. I've got a feeling you're going to get a workout soon. Not with that bastard Jordan, but with somebody new and a great fucker."

She combed out her long blonde hair with her fingers, letting it straggle down over her shoulders so some of it covered her breasts. It hung almost to her waist and was the color of soft gold.

She stretched, stood up and pulled on short bloomers, a white chemise and then a fancy flowered dress that she remembered tearing off herself sometime a day and a half ago.

She steadied herself when she took her first step, a bit dizzy. A day and a half without any food could do that to you. She had not needed food. The white tiger had provided her with the power that she needed. She grinned and walked barefooted out of her bedroom through a long hall, then down carpeted stairs with a hand-carved railing to the parlor.

Jordan stood there waiting, his hat in his hands, gratefully covering his crotch. Jordan always got a huge hard-on whenever he came to see her. He couldn't control it, she knew, but he'd have to get his erection taken down somewhere else. Jordan was a pig, and he knew it. He was also the best mine manager around.

When Jordan looked up, she was afraid he was going to bow down in homage. Instead his eyes widened as he watched the swing and sway of her breasts under the thin dress.

"Yes, Jordan. What do you have?"

"Some more evidence, Ma'am. I'm sure somebody is slipping into the mine at night, but I can't catch anyone since you said not to hire any more guards."

"What did you find, Jordan?"

"Footprints in the tunnel where there shouldn't be none. Then too, an ore car had been moved, and I found some digging at the end of level B down in tunnel twelve."

"Fine, Jordan, you watch it for me. If you catch anyone you tell them how dangerous it is down there. Anything else?"

"I don't suppose I could take you to dinner."

"No, Jordan, I don't suppose. Now get back to the mine."

Jordan turned and left, his hat still in his hands. As he turned she saw the profile of his erection sticking out of his work pants. Sometime it would be interesting just to see how big that pine log of his really was. She snorted at the idea, then went through the house to the kitchen.

The cook must have been alerted by Dolly because she had a big sandwich ready, two kinds of meat were heating up with some baked beans and three slices of home baked bread were cut to go with fresh churned butter and strawberry preserves. A plate and silverware had been set out at the kitchen table.

At the kitchen door, Cheyenne staggered again, caught herself and slid into the chair the cook held out.

"Ida, you're a sweet thing. I'd be dead years ago if it weren't for you. Coffee first, dear, about a quart, the hotter the better."

A half hour later, she had eaten everything in sight, changed into some man's jeans she had cut down for her and tucked a tight shirt into the pants tops. The belt had a wide buckle and she could feel her breasts pushing against the restricting shirt front. Good. Give the natives a thrill.

She remembered the flight of fancy and wonderment she had had last night, and it made her want to fly that same way again tonight. It felt so damn good!

But tonight was meeting time, the ceremony. She rubbed her crotch through the pants and smiled. Tonight was fuck-till-you-drop night, and she was hoping to find somebody interesting.

She walked in the garden. Her late husband had a soft spot for plants and fruit trees, planting every kind that would grow in the 5000 foot altitude. Every summer he had hired a man to carry water from the creek to water the plants. Then he dug a well and made it easier.

She could think in the garden, even after a few days on the white tiger. When she was on it her mind seemed so sharp that it would break. Plans, programs, projects came in thundering succession, but when she came down the next day she couldn't remember any of them. She needed to write them down. She tried it once but her writing was so slow that she threw the pad of paper away in disgust.

Now she had to reconstruct her secret society. It was getting ragged around the edges. Some of the women were getting nervous. Some of them were pregnant, but they were married. The men were all happy, all ten of them. She only had 21 members in the Society and Fellowship of the Blessed.

The Fellowship was strong. Not one person had dropped out, not even in the purification ceremony three weeks ago. That had been a highlight. The evil ones had been cleansed and the society had been strengthened.

For a moment Cheyenne broke out into raucous laughter. The whole idea of the fellowship had started out as a crazy, wild, unmentionable idea. She confided to a man she was bedding one night, and together they worked out some preliminary ideas and rules and practices. They each invited one new person to each meeting for three weeks, and suddenly they had eight members.

After that Cheyenne, as priestess of the fellowship, invited in who she thought would be most suitable. Nobody could participate who was over 35 years-old. Also no females under 14 were asked to join—except Dolly, her little Chinese slave. Dolly had loved the whole idea and provided them with the voodoo touches that Cheyenne wanted—the chicken blood ritual, the gris gris and the evil eye. A man from New York showed them the wonders of the pentagram, the powers of the white witches and some of the elements of devil worship. They even had a ram's head. Damn but it was fun. They had the whole fucking town cowed!

She even had the town's bigshot, Lud Halverson, in the group. Get him involved and he couldn't do anything to stop them. Hell, he was like a kid in a candy store. If you don't want to lick them, get them to join you. That's what Cheyenne always said.

Sure, half the people in town knew something wild went on in her house every Friday night, but most of them didn't want to know what it was. The ones who knew weren't saying. Anyone who tried to find out had a rude surprise that was embarrassing and downright painful.

Cheyenne had talked to Sheriff Gallon two days ago. No one had launched any protests or complaints. He had no word about the rituals they had recently. Nothing to worry about. The sheriff was a member of the society, of course.

Now if she could just sell the damn mine she could move to San Francisco and get into high society. Hell, she had as much money as most of them there did.

She picked a rose, a bright red blossom. When she snapped it off the bush, a thorn pricked her thumb. Cheyenne swore, threw down the rose and stomped it into the ground until it was little more than a stem and scattered bits of red blossom.

She shrugged and headed back for the castle. It wasn't really a castle, but it was the largest house in town with more than 30 rooms within three stories. All of the rituals, except those involving fire, were carried out in the seven rooms on the third floor. It had become their shrine, sealed off except for their Friday night celebrations of the spirit, of the body, of the mind, and of the everlasting most basic human drive—sexual gratification.

Cheyenne hurried back into the house. Tonight was meeting time. Her best 20 friends would be there on the third floor. The rule was that they came when it got dark, never before. No lamps were allowed on the third floor, only candles. There would be plenty of food and wine, hard liquor, tubs filled with river ice and bottles of beer.

She would lead the ritual as usual. The complicated rites of magic and voodoo and a little witchcraft made the pairings for the night. The pairings were always made according to the dictates of the higher gods. The All-Seeing-Eye dictated each step of the ceremony, and she was the only spokesperson for the All-Seeing-Eye.

Cheyenne giggled. The locals enjoyed it and kept coming back for more. What would the wild people in San Francisco do? She figured they would be twice as crazy for her rituals and ceremonies there as the hicks were here.

Cheyenne sat with her legs wide apart. She found a long, black cigar and lit it with a kitchen match. She pulled the harsh smoke into her lungs and then let it out slowly. Everything was ready and waiting. Stark-naked, Dolly would meet members of the society as usual at the front door. No one was allowed to touch her until they were inside the third floor doorway.

There Cheyenne met them in her long white robe. She never wore anything under it. She took another long drag on the cigar and smiled. Tonight would be a good one.

Three short blocks away, Ludwig George Halverson, a man of 48, sat in his back office in the Halverson Building considering his future. He owned all but four stores in town, including the largest ones—the bank, the community meeting hall, the Halverson General Store, and two saloons. There was no whorehouse in Timber Break, but there was a mother and daughter who provided personal services to those men in desperate need. They used their two-story house on B Street as their home and office.

There were not enough men in town for a real whorehouse or he would have set up one. Best thing he ever did was 14 years ago when he homesteaded this little valley and then established his store, stage stop and six room hotel. The town seemed to attract people.

Four years later when the silver strike boomed the little town reached more than 2000, but six months later it was back down to about 400 and the silver mine was turning out pure silver. The town lived on the mine.

Halverson drew a big breath and let it out slowly. He stood five-eight and always wore a black suit and black vest, a white shirt and a wide black tie. A matching black beard covered most of his face except for some judicious trimming on his cheeks.

The beard and dark brown eyes gave his face a roguish, foreboding look. That, coupled with the fact that he seldom smiled, had brought him the reputation of a cranky, no-nonsense skinflint who guarded his treasure with a vengeance and had the heart and soul of a miser who kept everyone at arms distance so he couldn't get hurt. It served his business interests well.

Halverson was not given to exercise or physical work, so he had developed into a somewhat chunky figure, weighing more than 180 pounds and swaying just a bit from side to side when he walked. He was married to a short, soft-spoken woman named Ruth, who he blamed for not bearing him any children. After 15 years of trying she had given up and never allowed him to touch her. They slept in separate beds, and Ruth toiled away in her small sewing room in the second biggest house in town. She was writing a novel, about a childless wife and how her husband and the whole town castigated her for it.

In the novel the lack of childbearing was entirely the husband's physical problem. He couldn't get any woman pregnant. The heroine in the novel at last had an affair with a young man and promptly became pregnant. When she was sure of her pregnancy, she made furious love to her husband and in time told him he had sired a son. She fooled him completely. Ruth wished she had enough nerve to try the same thing. Instead she spent all day pouring out her heart into the novel she was sure would never be published.

Now, in his office, Halverson studied a report about the mine. He had long been interested in the worked-out silver lode. Was it really worked-out, or had the great man himself, Winford Nance Barton, simply grown tired of the task of running the mine? That was a question that Winford would never answer.

Now on to more important things. Tonight was the ceremony. He would work his magic somehow and declare himself a partner with Cheyenne. It simply had to be. In a few months he would be free to marry again. Somehow poor Ruth seemed to get paler and weaker every day.

He lifted his brows and thought about the charms of Cheyenne. In the three months of the ceremony he had never been partnered with the lovely Cheyenne. Tonight was going to be the night, even if he had to pay off half the men on the third floor of the Barton mansion. Halverson laced his fingers behind his head and leaned back in his chair just thinking about it.

He had seen Cheyenne naked and knew of her surging breasts, so large and round and well-formed. The blonde thatch at her glory hole was no secret to him either. He had seen those pink, wanton lips but never touched them. Damn!

He pulled a string on the side of his desk which rang a small bell in his outer office. Gwendolyn, his secretary and office manager, knocked and came in. She was short and a little heavy, with shoulder-length dark hair, a soft hint of a moustache and doe eyes. She was unmarried and had worshipped Halverson for the four years she'd worked for him.

She looked at him and smiled.

"Is there something special I can do for you, Mr. Halverson?"

"Oh, yes, Gwen, there certainly is. Would you throw the bolt on the door, please?"

It was the signal. Gwen turned, bolted the door and walked over to Halverson. He had leaned further back in the chair and now spread his legs.

Gwendolyn went down on her knees between his spread legs and gently stroked his crotch.

"My goodness, Mr. Halverson, it seems you have some kind of a swelling here."

He nodded. "Show me, Gwen. Show them to me."

Gwendolyn unbuttoned her blouse and shrugged out of it, then she lifted her soft pink chemise over her head and thrust out her chest showing off her full breasts.

"Great tits, girl," he said. "Fine, fine tits. Bring them up here to me."

It was always the same routine, and she seemed to love it. She stood up so he could suckle her breasts. They were large, sagging just enough, and had ripe red nipples and paler areolas. As he sucked on her, Gwendolyn's hands busied themselves at his crotch, opening his fly, unbuckling his belt, spreading back his pants, then pulling out his erection.

"Oh, my, what a fine one," she said. Her voice shook with emotion, and her eyes went wide as they always did. Halverson lifted his mouth away from her breasts.

She sank back to her knees, then moved her head until she was over his throbbing erection.

"Oh, God, Gwen, do me right now! Suck me off till I go out of my skull."

Gwen closed her eyes, settled down over his large cock and then felt his hips start to move up and down. Gwen let out a moan, pushed one hand down to her own crotch and spread her legs, finding the softness where she already was wet and wanting. Her finger found the small node, and she twanged it each time he humped into her mouth.

She moaned again and tried to look up at him, but all she could see was his hairy chest under his shirt and the pounding of his hips.

Gwen closed her eyes. Deep down she knew that this was the most she would ever have of Lud Halverson, but for now it was enough. Maybe sometime later, he would want to be inside of her again. Gwen settled down to doing exactly what her employer wanted her to do. The ten dollar bonus he always gave her would not be unwelcome either, but he must know she didn't need the bonus. She closed her eyes again and increased the pressure on his plunging prick.

Chapter Three

Spur McCoy eased away from the hot kiss and looked down at the pretty girl. Jessica Edwards grinned, spun away from him and walked from the closed back porch into the kitchen. She stood behind a chair and watched him.

"Mr. McCoy, that was just a sample. I want you to know that I'm smitten with you, but I'm not the kind of girl to tear off my clothes and take you to bed the first chance we get."

"Like now, the first chance," McCoy said. He had followed her into the middle of the kitchen but made no further move toward her.

"I figured you were a gentleman and that I could give you a small sample of me and not get into any serious trouble. I was right, wasn't I?"

McCoy laughed and nodded. "You did have me going there for a minute. You are one sexy lady. I admit I was thinking what you would look like with your clothes off."

Jessica turned her face, and he didn't know if she were blushing or grinning. "Mr. McCoy, that's not the kind of talk I had planned on having. We are going to the parlor and sit down six feet apart and talk. Yes, talk. I want to know all about you and what you're really doing in town. A man who's so good with a rifle can't be here for the clear mountain air and the cultural delights of Timber Break."

She walked into the parlor and turned to see that he followed her. Jessica sat in an upholstered chair and pointed to a matching one four feet from her own. He sat down.

"Now we talk. Just why are you in this poky little town, anyway, Mr. McCoy?"

"Miss Edwards, since we're already such good friends, and you've kissed me not once but twice and pushed yourself hard against me, I think we should use our first names. I'm Spur. May I call you Jessica?"

When she laughed it delighted him. She was young and pretty and had a slender sexy body he wanted to undress. "Mr. McCoy, I allow first names only after I've kissed a man three times. Now, why are you here?"

"Mostly to find out why this town is so unfriendly and so clannish. It's like a huge conspiracy not to to let anyone who isn't a native be a part of the community."

Jessica nodded. "I've noticed a little of that. The ladies in the shop call me 'the new girl' and never even inquire about my name. It is strange. I asked Aunt Wilda about it, and she shushed me, said it was no business of mine and she wanted to forget all about it."

"Forget about what?"

"I don't have the faintest idea. Aunt Wilda is not a woman you want to question. She's strong-willed and has made her own way after her husband died ten years ago, leaving her with three children."

"I'd like to talk to her."

"Why?"

He watched her a moment, then waggled a finger at her. "Promise me you won't tell anyone about what I'm about to reveal to you. It's important, probably more vital than we realize. This must be our dark secret. All right?"

She bobbed her head, and he liked the way it made her breasts jiggle.

"Yes, I promise. This sounds exciting."

"Let's hope it's not too exciting. I'm here looking for a man who seems to have vanished right off the face of the earth. I'm not sure if he left Timber Break, but I know that he arrived."

"Is he an important man, famous, something like that?"

"Famous, no. Important? Well, let's just say he's a friend of a famous man who wants him found."

"He hired you to find him?"

McCoy nodded. "In a way, yes. You don't need to know that. It's my job to find him, but I'm not sure who I can trust in this little town."

"I wouldn't trust anybody who lives here. Maybe somebody who is going through or who has just arrived, like me. Actually I'm flattered."

"I need a friendly ear here in town. The stage drivers go in and out, but I doubt if any of them are close-mouthed. Fact is I talked to some of them earlier today, but now I'm not sure where to go. As for the sheriff I'll have to see if he's safe."

"I think you can talk to my Aunt Wilda. She's a good Christian woman. I'm sure she wouldn't do anything evil or illegal. Do you want me to see if she'll talk to you?"

"How would you go about it?"

"I don't know. Any suggestions?"

"You could say we came in on the stage together. Maybe I knocked down some man who insulted you, something like that. Maybe you promised me a home cooked dinner. Yeah, that could do it. Of course, Aunt Wilda would do the cooking. What do you think?"

Jessica giggled. "I could pretend that you practically saved my honour and reputation. Yes, I like that. Aunt Wilda would almost have to invite you to supper. I'll work around to it tomorrow, and maybe tomorrow night we can get together."

The chiming clock on the mantle struck eight. Jessica looked at it and fidgeted.

"Maybe you better leave. It would spoil our story if she found you here."

"The back door?"

She grinned and nodded. Jessica led the way through the kitchen to the small back porch that was closed in against the blustering wind from the Idaho mountains.

At the back door she stopped and turned. McCoy stood just in front of her. She put her arms around his neck and pulled his face down to hers. He saw in the dim light that her eyes were closed as she kissed him, but this time she didn't let her breasts touch him.

He heard her give a soft little sigh as the kiss ended. Her eyes snapped open and she eased away from him.

"Now you can call me Jessica," she said.

McCoy chuckled. "Good. Jessica, could I have one more good night kiss?"

"Absolutely not," she said smiling. She leaned toward him, pushed her breasts against his chest and reached up for his lips. The kiss was soft, tender and gentle and made McCoy think of many things, but not one of them was sexy at all. They were dangerous things like a small house with a white picket fence around it and roses near the walk and this pretty girl waving at him from the doorway.

He finished the kiss with a gentle hug and let her go.

"Now, that, Spur McCoy, was a fine way to say hello, not goodbye. But it better be goodbye. You stop by about noon tomorrow and I'll let you know what progress I've made with Aunt Wilda. I think she'll come around."

McCoy touched her shoulder, then walked down the two steps into the Idaho night. He looked up. It was so clear that the stars seemed like they were at the end of his arm. He checked two of the constellations, then found the big dipper and the north star. Good. It always made him feel better to know where the north star was.

McCoy found himself smiling as he headed for the business section of the village. Jessica was delightful, but he wasn't here to enjoy a beautiful young woman. He was here to find the colonel, who might be calling himself the general now. Who else in town might know something and be willing to talk?

The town had two saloons, but the barkeeps were too obvious. They might know a lot, but chances are they would be as close-mouthed as the rest of the residents.

"Who the hell else?" he asked outloud. A drunk leaning against a building looked at him with red-shot and bleary eyes.

"Not me, brother!" the drunk said.

McCoy moved on past, then he nodded. Of course, he should have thought of it before. He turned in at the next saloon, the Grubstake, and bought a beer from the keg. McCoy stood at the short bar watching the patrons who were mostly locals he decided. Two card games were going on, both poker. The 21 table was deserted.

The barkeep wiped the glossy surface without looking at it. He stared at McCoy and then came down to him.

"You new in town." It was a statement.

"Yep, came in yesterday. Working down at the livery."

"Not much of a job."

"Not many jobs around. You know where I can get a better one?"

"In Boise."

"Don't like Boise. Too big, too noisy, too many damned people."

The apron grunted.

"Need a bouncer in here?"

"Look like we get any trouble? I can handle anything that happens. Got me a pool cue cut off and a sawed-off shotgun."

"Should take care of it." McCoy finished his mug of beer and pushed the glass down the counter to the barkeep's waiting hand.

"Know where a man can get some relief around here? Ain't seen a single whorehouse in town."

The apron snorted. "Cause we ain't got one. All we got is Hattie and her daughter Pris. They service the whole damn town. Hattie had the clap a month ago. Don't know if she's working yet or not."

"Her daughter up to a poking?"

"Always has been."

McCoy edged a silver dollar across the counter, and it vanished into the apron's quick hand.

"Find their house a block down on Main Street. It's the white one with the red trim. The trim was Pris's idea. She's a good-sized girl, gives you a good ride."

Spur nodded, leaned against the bar for a minute, then eased away and strolled outside.

He easily found the whorehouse where a soft light in the front window evidently indicated it was open for business.

McCoy went up to the door, rapped once then pushed it open. Beyond the door he found a small entryway, with a hallway opening off it and a door to the left. A bright coal oil lamp burned on a table.

A woman came down the hall. "Walk right in, big spender. We're always open." She came into the light of the lamp and McCoy figured she was the mother, Hattie.

"You over the clap yet, Hattie?"

"How do you know." She stopped and shrugged. "Fuck, no, but my sweet little girl is clean. Not busy right now. You interested?"

"I don't buy no pig in a poke."

"Pris is no damned pig. You go down the hall and look in that second door and see for yourself. Three dollars for a piece that young. She's just seventeen."

"Two dollars and everybody knows Pris is twenty-three and bored out to double size."

Hattie grinned, showing one missing tooth in front.

"Damnation, how do you pricks get so smart? Hell, go take a look. She'll do you good. No free one, no matter what she says. Poor girl gets carried away sometimes."

As McCoy walked past her she reached out and patted his rump.

"Hey, sugar, if Pris ain't woman enough for you, Hattie is always here and waiting." She laughed and spread her legs. McCoy laughed with her, then went on down the hall to the door Hattie had indicated and knocked.

A moment later the door opened and a round, sweet face peered out.

"Yes?"

"Miss Pris?"

"The same, best in all of Idaho."

"I'd like to talk to you for a few minutes."

"That what you call it? Hell, don't make no matter to me. Call it whatever you want to, if'n you got the three dollars."

"Two dollars, Pris. Fact is, I come here to talk, not to make use of your talents."

"Oh, shit!" Pris opened the door to reveal a generously fleshy girl who now did look only 17, but he was sure she was somewhere past 20. She wore a thin silk robe that he could see right through, showing every roll of fat and her ponderous swaying breasts. Pris wasn't just chunky; she was gloriously, unredemptively fat. He kept thinking 250 pounds. He wouldn't be far off. She was no more than five-feet-three.

"Suppose you don't like fat whores, either."

"Didn't say that. You want to talk for two dollars worth, or are you independently rich?"

She motioned him inside, closed the door, and went around him and dropped on the bed. He was sure it had been reinforced to stand her weight.

"What do you want to talk about?"

"People."

"Hell, I can tell you about them. Horny old men and gossipy old bitches who think they're Christ himself."

"You don't socialize much with the women folk of Timber Break."

"I do, but they don't. I go to some socials, and they all leave. Happened twice so now I just don't go nowhere. Sit here and mope or lay here and fuck. That's about it for me."

"But you do get to know some of the men right well, I'd guess."

"Oh, yes. Knew the richest man in town for two years. Then he hooked up with some town woman who he's fucking regular so he don't need me. Bet she costs him a sight more than a lousy two bucks a week."

"No bet, you'd win. Got me another question. Why are folks so stand-offish around here? Seems like everybody is ready to slam a door in my face."

"You been asking questions?"

"Not a one. Work down at the livery. Started yesterday. Figured the most popular woman in town would know the lay of the land around here."

"It's all mountains and meadows, but mostly snowbanks. Best for you to just trail on out of town. No future here for a man like you. I'd hate to see any harm come to you. Gawd, but you're a handsome man. Don't think I've ever done me a gent who looks so good as you and has such a powerful, lean and ready body." She let the front of the robe slip open to show off one huge breast with a nipple the size of his thumb.

"Hey, you want a free one? No charge. Worth it for me to see that big whanger of yours and find out how fucking good you are with it behind that pile driving ass of yours."

"Like I said, I just want to talk."

"What's the matter? You don't like pussy?"

"I like girls, usually a little too much."

"Then what's the matter with me? You not a tit man, fine. I'll show you a pussy that will send you into the shivers." She slid the robe off and lay back on the bed, lifting her knees and spreading them to show him a pink slot three inches long.

"Now, cowboy, is that a cunt to ride the range in or not? Come on, just a quick one. A free one for you."

"Then you'll answer some questions for me?"

"Hey, get me hot enough and I'll talk your whanger off. No lie. You get my cunt hot and juicy and I forget everything I ever knew about keeping quiet."

McCoy unbuckled his gunbelt and let it slide to the floor. He opened his pants buckle, and Pris squealed in delight. She sat up and pulled his shirt out of his pants and stripped down the town britches, then his short underwear.

"Gawd! I think I've died and done gone straight to heaven. How did you get such a big whanger when most men brag about a six-incher?"

She pulled him over her, clamping him with her knees and working him down slowly until he meshed, and in one powerful stroke he jolted into her until his pelvic bones slammed into her rolls of fat.

"Oh, damn!" Pris shrieked. "You hit something in there that no fucker ever touched before. Oh, Christ, this is going to be the finest one of my life".

He stroked three times, then stopped. Her hips pounded against his and kept going when he paused.

"Pris, what is everyone in this town afraid of? I can smell the fear. Nobody will talk to me. Every stranger in town gets the cold shoulder. What's the big secret here, anyway?"

"Don't know what you're talking about. Come on, don't stop now. I need you slamming into my cunt!"

He stroked twice more then stopped.

"Pris, who runs things in this town, the mine owner?"

"Hell, no, he died. His damn widow owns the mine, but it's shut down."

"Then who runs the town?"

"Halverson. Fucking Lud Halverson. He owns the town. Used to be his homestead. He proved it up and built this town. Sells lots, owns most of the stores and the bank. Bucking-fucking big shot Halverson who got his own pussy on the side."

"So he's married?"

"Damn right. She knows he fucks around but doesn't care. Folks say her pussy dried up years ago anyway. She's so tight she can't even piss without screaming."

"I can understand a man owning a town, but how can he keep everyone afraid, scared even to talk to strangers?"

"You better go ask him. I fer sure ain't gonna tell you. Not even two or three fucks would be worth that. Come on, poke me, damn you. I answered your questions."

McCoy drove in again, punching into the fat girl and pounding her hard until she squealed in anticipation. Then a moment later she exploded with a series of long climaxes that nearly unseated him. She rattled and jolted and shook like an aspen leaf in a windstorm.

He held back, marveling at the variety of her reactions. Sometimes she brayed like a mule; sometimes she moaned and mewed like a small kitten. She ended each of the climaxes with a high keening that sent shivers up his spine.

When she came down from the last one, McCoy lifted her ankles, put her thick legs on his shoulders, and rode up on her until her thighs nearly touched her face. Then he blasted at her a dozen times before he screeched in pure joy and erupted with a roar as he pounded a dozen times at her, releasing his seed and planting it as deeply as he could.

Then he let her legs off his shoulders and dropped on her, pushing her deep into the featherbed. They lay there for five minutes before she began to wiggle.

She stared at him. "Christ, I ain't come like that in five years. Not since my second fuck from that no-good preacher's kid. Damn, he was good with his whanger, but a bust at everything else. Town council finally ran him out of the place, and he joined the army from what the sheriff knew."

She watched him as he rolled away from her and they both sat up.

"You don't know what everyone in town is so afraid of?" he asked.

Pris stroked his inner thigh. "Like I said, big whanger, you go and ask Halverson himself. Then you won't get no wrong answers."

"Then he'd probably ride me out of town on a rail or have me shot in the back. It looks like one of those kinds of secrets. What can I do for you so you'll tell me?"

She squeezed up her eyes for a moment, then shook her head. "No, not even a tongue job would make me tell you. I got more respect for my skin than that. We had one guy here in town who talked too much and he got . . ." She stopped.

"Oh, Lord, I almost done it that time. Now you get out of here before I make a big mistake. Probably already told you too much, but who would believe I'd even know anything? You get out of here, but you be careful, you hear. Hate to hear that a big whanger like yours got himself killed."

Chapter Four

Later that same evening, just as the sky faded from pale dusk into the black of night, heavily draped figures arrived at the big castle where Cheyenne Barton lived. They came singly, rang the bell and were let inside.

After 20 individuals arrived the lamp on a small table on the front porch of the mansion sputtered out.

Inside the scene was much different.

Dolly greeted each arrival. The small Chinese girl stood straight and tall and naked as she welcomed each visitor by name and showed the way up to the third floor.

The women smiled at Dolly, while the men petted and caressed her bare breasts a moment, then grinned and hurried upstairs.

All of the visitors had been draped with enough outer garments to disguise their identities, but once inside they pulled off the heavy coats and capes and smiled and joked as they walked up the staircase.

The third floor was different from the rest of the house. One door led off the stairway. On it was a round pentagram painted in bright red, with all of the signs and symbols usually found there. Past the pentagram, a long hall stretched out with six open doors along it.

As the people came, they gathered in the first room, the council room, for the ceremony. The people took off their outer wraps as they entered and deposited them on a table, then sat in chairs in a circle around the room.

The front of the room held an altar which was done all in black with three large red candles burning on it. They were placed in a triangle. Smoke from burning incense drifted across the room.

Eleven of the 21 chairs in the room were painted black and grouped on one side of the circle; the other ten chairs, which were red, were on the other side. The women took the red chairs as they arrived and the men sat in the black ones. One of the chairs was white and taller than the rest, but no one sat in that one.

The women who arrived were young, twenties and thirties; the men were also in their thirties with one or two in their forties.

White butcher paper covered the area between the chairs. It had been cut and taped together to form a perfect circle. No one stepped on the paper. They came to their chairs from the back, pulled them out, stepped inside and brought the chair back in behind them.

Within a few minutes all of the chairs except the high white one were filled. The people watched the door, and a moment later Cheyenne appeared. She wore a long black robe that tied around her neck and came to the floor. It billowed as she walked in. All talk ceased as she sat in the high white chair and looked over the gathering.

"Great is the power of the ram," Cheyenne said.

The 20 around the circle repeated her words.

"Six times six is eleven, forty-three and two are seven," Cheyenne said. The 20 voices repeated her words in a monotone. She said the same words three times and the voices echoed her.

When she stood and nodded Dolly appeared at the side of the group and handed Cheyenne a live chicken. Dolly held the head of the chicken as Cheyenne used a sharp knife to cut the chicken's head off.

Blood spurted out, and Cheyenne swung the chicken around and around as she walked over the white paper on the floor. The spattering blood caught her robe and bare feet, but most of the blood gushed and dripped on the white paper. The members of the group stared in amazement at the bloodletting. All had seen it before several times, but still the blood ritual thrilled and excited them.

One of the women started moaning, but others touched her and kept her quiet.

Cheyenne dropped the dead chicken in the middle of the paper and lifted both her bloody hands over her head. She put on a black mask that covered most of her face and began to chant.

"Blackness comes, and blackness goes. Helon, Taul, Varf, Heon, Homoonoreum, Clemalth, Serugeath, Alga, Tesasibuana, Casoly!"

She breathed the names of the great devil spirits she invoked. The heavy aroma of incense increased along with a wafting of smoke.

"I petition these, oh great spirits. Welcome to our gathering and may we live and work in the light of thy blackness. May all come with the will to do the ceremony."

She removed the black mask and cast it outside the circle. She unbuttoned two places on the robe and let it fall to the bloody papers inside the circle. Under the robe she was naked as all there knew she must be.

"Come, sisters," she said. Cheyenne moved outside the circle and began walking around it. The women in the group arose from their chairs and followed her. They chanted softly as they circled the chairs, each one removing items of clothing and dropping them on the chairs. After three times around the chairs, all 11 women were naked.

Cheyenne stared at the nude women. None were as busty as she was. Flames danced behind her glittering eyes. The tiger was roaring tonight. She made a motion with her hands.

"Each one, choose one," she said. "Beware of the female. The female of the species is twice as deadly as the male. Tonight, the females will choose."

Shrieks of delight shrilled from the women who stood ready on their side of the circle.

"Go!" Cheyenne said. The women stormed around and over and across the circle aiming at the man they wanted. Cheyenne watched them a moment, then became aware that someone stood next to her.

She stared down slightly to find Lud Halverson reaching for her breasts.

"Choose me tonight," he said softly. "We have many things to talk about." His hands touched her breasts, caressing and petting them until she thought she would burst.

"Yes," she said softly, caught his hand and ran down the hall to the last room on the left. They were the first ones there. Three mattresses lay on the floor. Cheyenne sat down and felt the tiger clawing at her. Everything was moving so slowly for her. Why didn't he get his clothes off faster? What was he waiting for?

He bent and kissed her breasts, then sucked on them. He pulled her toward him on the mattress. At last his clothes were off. He looked paunchy, sloppy, gut fat. His flesh was soft and pale. Only his eyes glistened.

"I've been waiting for this for weeks," he said rolling her on top of him.

"Yes, yes, you said many things to talk about. What?"

"We should become partners and unite the richest man and woman in town."

"Not possible. I'm richer." Why didn't he get on with it so they could meet again and change partners in the changing ceremony?

"I'm far richer than you are," she said.

She barely felt him roll her onto her back, spread her legs and enter her. There was no thrill, only the fact that it had taken so long, and there were so many young men waiting with such big whangers.

"I'll buy your mine. Worthless, but I'll give you fifty thousand dollars for it."

"Not enough."

He groaned, humped her harder and faster, then bellowed like an enraged bull and collapsed on top of her. She pushed him off and stood up.

"Changing ceremony," she said. The tiger made it more important to change quickly. Everyone was so slow tonight. She giggled, knowing it was the tiger; the white tiger could do it every time. What a marvelous feeling! She was ten feet tall! She was the richest woman in the world! She was the best lover in all the universe! She could have any man in Idaho that she wanted. The governor? Easy.

"I don't want to go to the changing ceremony," the man beside her said. She had to think who he was. Yes, the old man, Halverson. Though he was 48 years-old, they needed him in the ceremony for security.

"Changing ceremony," she said. He shook his head, grabbed her by her thighs and pulled her back to the mattress. There was another couple on the mattress closest to the door. The woman was on her knees with the man trying to enter her from behind. He was so slow.

Cheyenne fell to the mattress, and the man lay on top of her.

"Look, we don't have to go changing. Let's just stay here and fuck and talk. I'm not going to be married forever. I want to marry you, make it legal, have you every night. Show you how a real man can keep you satisfied. Keep your little pussy all to myself and not spread it all over the county."

She rolled away from him and stood up. He came up on his knees, pleading with her.

"No. I'm in charge and I'll go to changing if I want to."

When he made a grab at her, she lashed out with her foot. The top of her bare foot crashed against the side of his inner thigh and powered upward, jolting into his limp penis and continuing to smash one of Lud Halverson's testicles upward until it hit his pelvic bones. The force wasn't enough to crush the testicle, but it brought an immediate wail of indescribable pain from Halverson. He fell backward, drew up his legs to his chest in a protective ball and screamed in agony. Halverson wouldn't be changing after all.

Cheyenne looked at him for a moment with indifference, then walked out of the room and down the hall to the assembly room where they had met. Early arrivals had moved the chairs back against the walls. The paper and chicken and chicken blood had been cleaned up. About half the couples were back, talking and petting, waiting for her.

Cheyenne went to the middle of the room. "Changing time," she said, and the men and women formed two circles with the women in the middle. The men began a chant that went from one to four and back to one again. The women moved clockwise and the men counterclockwise. Cheyenne loved this part of the game. Whoever you stopped opposite when the chanting stopped was your new partner. It was going to be a fine night. The white tiger agreed.

An hour later, Spur McCoy left the white house where Pris lived and headed for a saloon. He needed a drink.

He needed several drinks. Something strange and dangerous had taken over this town. He had to find out who or what it was. Whatever it was probably had done something fatal to Colonel Potter.

How the hell was he going to find out without just coming out and identifying himself? Should he marshall the sheriff into his force and start kicking some butts? He had to try the more prudent method first. The only trouble was that he was fast running out of people to talk to.

McCoy bought into a nickel limit poker game and played for an hour. No one there was talking. He didn't even get the chance to ask. He lost a dollar and moved on to the bar where he asked for a mug of beer and watched the small crowd at the bar. With the town's main industry gone, there wasn't a lot of spare cash floating around. Most of the people in town had their own garden and grew food. They had root cellars and dried what they could and tried to preserve it any way they could for the winter.

He spotted a man at a back table, playing a game of solitaire. Nothing about the man indicated that he was of the higher social order. He looked like a drunk. Just might be the right man.

Spur sat beside him, put a fresh mug of beer down in front of him and offered his hand.

"Spur McCoy. Don't think I've met you."

"Course not. Nobody meets Shorty Clawson unless they want something from him. Got no money, got no bottle, got no woman, got no house, not even a damned place to sleep." He looked up through bloodshot eyes. "What 'n hell you say your handle was?"

"Spur McCoy. I just bought you a beer."

"If you're trying to get me drunk, it won't work. I been drunk now for two days."

"Why?"

"Why not?"

Spur laughed. "Good question. You lived here long?"

"Drunk or sober?"

"Both."

"Long about five years. Used to work in the mine."

"Why is this town so unfriendly?"

"Why not? Why be friendly? Let me finish this beer and I'll tell you about unfriendly. This guy came to town, a damn colonel in the army." The man lifted the mug of beer and didn't stop drinking until he had emptied it. He belched, then fell forward on the table and passed out.

McCoy shook his shoulder, but the man didn't move. He lifted Shorty's hand and dropped it. Somebody came to the table and McCoy looked up at a small man with a mug of beer in his hand.

"Hell, he's done it again. No use trying to wake him up, friend. He'll be out the rest of the night and half of tomorrow. Just can't hold his liquor anymore."

The man shuffled off to another table and sat down, nursing the beer so it would last.

McCoy scowled at the drunk in front of him and went back to the bar. He finished his beer there, cast around for a new man to talk to, but found nobody he figured he could trust.

The barkeep tapped his empty beer mug, but McCoy shook his head. "Looks like I've about paid the piper for tonight," he said and headed for the door.

Before he made it to the swinging doors, two big men stood up and met him. They didn't exactly block his way but one of them nodded.

"You have a good talk with Shorty Clawson at that back table?" he asked.

McCoy snorted. "That old drunk? Hardly. He told me he knew where I could get a good job. All I'd have to do was buy him a beer. So I buy him the beer and he chugs it down, burps and passes out on me. I only been here two days, but this is a damn unfriendly little town."

The other man, the larger one who stood as tall as McCoy but weighed 60 pounds heavier, pushed up close to McCoy.

"In that case, stranger, why don't you just catch the next stage out of town?"

"Why?" McCoy backed up two steps and let his right hand hover over the butt of his .45 Colt. "I'll tell you why, stranger. Whenever an asshole like you starts pushing me around, I start pushing back. You got a piece on your hip. Go ahead and use it if you've got the balls."

The big man's eyes went wide, and he looked at his partner. There was confusion in his face, and he lifted both hands well away from his six-gun. He looked at McCoy, the tied-down holster, the well-used look of the leather, then the hand that hovered over the iron. The first man took up the slack.

"Hey, we were just funnin' you, stranger. We worry about Shorty, that's all. Want to get him to quit drinking so much. This new job angle is something we can warn people about. No offense. My brother here gets a little pushy sometimes, but forget it. No hard feelings?"

McCoy kept his hand where it was. "Never was. Just remind this brother of yours that the bigger a man is, the farther he has to fall and the harder he hits. Now, if the two of you don't mind, I have some business to attend to."

Spur pushed past the bigger man, shouldering him to the side, and strode out the bar door, showing them his back and demonstrating to them that he was not afraid of them.

Outside he darted to the side of the bar door and waited. Neither of the big men came out. McCoy let out a short sigh of relief. He'd have to find out who those two were and who they worked for. They were too stupid to have anything going on their own. They were hired muscle. That was another piece of the puzzle he had to figure out. Just how did these two fit in with Colonel Potter's disappearance?

Chapter Five

Spur McCoy walked across the street from the Grub-stake Saloon and leaned against the closed hardware store wall. He watched the drinking emporium. Fifteen minutes later the two big men came out, walked down the street to the town's other saloon and went in.

McCoy crossed the street and went into the Grub-stake. He found the same barman he had slipped the silver dollar to earlier. He nodded, and the man came down the bar. McCoy spoke quietly so no one else could hear him.

"Who were those clowns who hassled me when I left before?" he asked.

The barkeep worked on polishing the shining bar in front of McCoy.

"We call them the dumbbell twins. Work for Halverson, gent who owns the town. Not the best liked pair in Timber Break."

McCoy snorted. "They won't get my vote for city council. Just wondered." Spur paused a moment, nodded at the barman and left the saloon. Tomorrow he'd have a talk with this Halverson. If he owned the whole town, he might know what was going on. More important, he might not be afraid of anyone and willing to talk.

The next morning, McCoy found out where Halverson had his office. It was right next to the Timbers Bank in the only brick building in town.

The outer office was neat and practical yet at the same time had a touch of class. It had a carpet on the floor and an oak desk where a rather plump woman in her early thirties sat. She stared at McCoy for a moment, then smiled.

"Good morning. May I help you?"

"That you can, girl. I'm needing to see Mr. Halverson on a matter of some urgency."

"I'd have to know exactly what the urgency is."

McCoy had stopped in front of her desk. He could see she was more than a little plump; she bordered on being fat. She had a pretty face not affected by the surplus of pounds elsewhere.

McCoy grinned. "The urgency, Miss, is mine, not his. I'm hunting a job, a position if possible. I was wondering if the gentleman would have a place for a man with my talents."

The woman smiled. Spur saw her move in the chair as if she were uncomfortable. "Your name?"

"Spur McCoy. Right now I'm working for the livery. My urgency is to find a better paying, more interesting job."

The woman shook her head. "I'm sorry, but Mr. Halverson doesn't handle employment for his various enterprises. Each business or operation does that for itself. You might check with the store managers."

Just then the door behind opened and a man came through. He was five-foot-nine, on the chunky side himself and maybe 50 years old, Spur estimated. He took a chance.

"Mr. Halverson, my name is Spur McCoy, and I'm in town two days working at the livery and looking for a better job. Any openings in your businesses?"

"I told you, Mr. Halverson doesn't handle . . ."

Halverson put his hand on the woman's shoulder. She stopped talking at once and shivered slightly.

"That's right, McCoy. I don't do the hiring, just the firing. What line of work are you in?"

"Almost anything, Mr. Halverson."

The merchant came around the desk and looked at McCoy. He eyed the tied down .45 holster and nodded. "I see you can handle a gun right well, otherwise there'd be no reason for you to tie down the bottom of your holster that way. I've heard it can make the difference between beating a man to the draw and getting yourself killed. That true?"

"It's happened, Mr. Halverson. I ain't looking for gun work. Just keep the piece for my own protection."

"Like if somebody were to call you out or find out your real name and the rep you built say in Kansas or Texas?"

"Nothing like that. I'm just an ordinary man trying to make a living."

Halverson smiled. "Wouldn't expect you to admit to no kind of a reputation for being a gunhand. Come to think of it, I just might have some work for you. You must be the new man in town a pair of my people talked to last night in the Grubstake Saloon."

"You mean the dumbbell twins. Yeah, they got a little frisky with me. They kind of remind me of a loose cannon rolling around the deck of a fighting ship at sea. Can cause the friendly forces all sorts of trouble."

Halverson nodded. "I've been told that before. You're probably right, but out here in the wilderness of Idaho, we have to work with the talent that we have." He frowned a moment, then nodded. "Come into my office. We need to talk."

McCoy followed Halverson into the office and took the chair indicated across from a large desk with half a dozen different stacks of papers. He tried to read the man's character but had little to go on. Rich and powerful, but did he have anything to do with the disappearance of Colonel Potter?

Halverson peaked his fingers and looked over them. "I'd say you've done your share of gun work. Won't be any of that here in Timber Break. You must know this is my town. It all rests on my original homestead. I've sold off parts of it, but most of the town is mine—lock, stock and chimney sweep.

"Now, from time to time I do have some problems with renters, merchants and employees. True, I've been using Kirk and Kerry as my—what shall I call them?—my enforcers. Granted neither one is too bright. I'm not sure if they could hit the floor if they were standing on it with their six-guns. However, the pair of them is impressive when they take my message to somebody behind in his rent."

Halverson stood, walked around the desk and stared through a window at the town.

"Maybe it's time I changed my image and came on a little less strong, more of a gentle and understanding man. Yes, something to think about. Could be big changes in this town. No telling when somebody might discover new silver in the mountains. The town could boom up to five thousand souls again in six months. I'm still on the ground floor. I own most of the land five miles each way up and down the valley."

He came back to the desk. "Yes, Mr. McCoy, I think I'll hire you. Ten dollars a week. Report here every morning at eight and see what jobs I have given Gwen here for you to do."

McCoy stood. "I don't work for ten dollars a week. Make it twenty and you have a new hand."

Halverson chuckled. "You're hired at twenty. I would have gone to twenty-five. I like your style, McCoy. One rule. I don't want any of the locals busted up or killed. First rule of my business. I live with these folks, and I won't tolerate any brutality."

"Understood. I can start work tomorrow morning. A few things to get cleaned up first."

"But you're just new to town."

"True, and I need some new clothes and a better place to stay. Can you recommend a boarding house?"

Twenty minutes later McCoy checked out of the hotel and stopped by the back door of the women's wear store. Jessica responded to his knock.

"I'm moving to the Schatzman Boarding House," he told her.

Jessica nodded. "Good. Hotels cost too much."

"I'm also working for Mr. Halverson as a kind of jack of all trades."

"Including gun work?"

"Doubt it. He's playing his role of benevolent king and doesn't want to get too rough with his neighbors."

"You making any progress on your search?"

"None. But I have hopes. Keep your ears open for me."

"I will." She touched his arm, reached up quickly and kissed his cheek, then closed the door.

As soon as McCoy left the office, Halverson called in a thin man with a full beard and a soft cap.

"Follow him. Find out where he goes, what he does, and where he lives if you can. He could be at Schatzman's. Get out of here."

The man bobbed his head twice, grinned, showing stubs of blackened teeth, and hurried out the door.

Halverson frowned. His two big men had reported the meeting with McCoy. They didn't know his name, but they knew how he tied his gun low. Both were probably lucky to be alive. If McCoy was who he said he was, he would be a good ace in the hole for Halverson enterprises—a real gunman who could do gun work the way it should be done.

He looked at his watch. Where had the morning gone? Time to go home for a special lunch with his wife, Ruth. He squinted. It has been almost two months. It shouldn't take long now.

Ten minutes later in his home, Lud Halverson fixed lunch for Ruth. She wanted only a poached egg and toast and sat up in bed for the food. He brought it along with a glass of milk.

"No milk today," Ruth said.

"Now you know you need the nourishment. Good for your bones. You have this glass this noon and that will be enough for today."

He had mixed the powder into her milk until it was completely dissolved. There was no chance she could taste it. The build-up had been gradual, and any day now it could happen. She looked weaker today.

Ruth drank most of the milk and ate the egg and toast. Then she clutched his hand.

"Lud, I'm so lucky to have you to help me. I'm going to get over this sick spell and then things will be like they used to be. You'll see."

Her hand felt like a claw to him. He had to steel himself not to pull away from her.

"You just rest now, Ruth, and get well. I'll just take these dishes and put them in the kitchen for the maid. Then I better get back to work. Has the girl been reading to you?"

"Yes. Some interesting stories from the maga- zines."

"That's nice, dear."

He waved and hurried out of the house. She did look worse today. A week perhaps, then it would be all over and he could start his courtship of Cheyenne. He felt an erection even as he thought about her. Last night had been fantastic. What a body that woman had! She also knew how to use it, even when she was half out of her head with the white tiger. He looked down, hoping that his hard-on didn't show. What a night that had been!

He had never been with a woman like her—such large breasts and that tight little hole and such a pounding, grinding ass! And so tall, almost six feet of woman, so perfectly formed. It was heaven for a few minutes for him. He touched his forehead and sensed the sweat there. He would have to find time to invite Gwen back to his office this afternoon. Once was never enough. Damn, but last night was one he would never forget.

In the office, Leonard waited for Halverson. Leonard had been teasing Gwen. Her neck was red from blushing, and a touch of perspiration showed on her upper lip. Leonard had been teasing her about making love again. She was hotter than a blacksmith's forge. Too bad he couldn't satisfy her right then.

He grunted at Leonard and waved him into his office. When the door closed, Halverson looked sharply at Leonard.

"You teasing that poor girl again, Leonard?"

The other man grinned. He was slender and tall, a beanpole of a man with soft brown hair, a good smile and sharp features that made you think of a hawk.

"Teasing her? Yeah, some. Damn, but I bet she'd be a good humper in the afternoon. Different from the whores, you know. Sort of shy and wondering and then you get her heated up just right and she gives you a great ride."

"I wouldn't know. It's strictly business here. You came for something important? I told you not to come to the office."

"Yeah, I know, but it is important. I figure we might have found something. Not sure yet, but it's gonna take at least two more night's work. I could use another man."

"You have one in mind who can keep his mouth shut?"

"Yeah, my brother-in-law. I told him what's what and that I'd kill him if he let slip a word. He's not real smart but he's big and strong and can move a lot of dirt and rocks. He won't say a word."

"Take him with you. It looks promising?"

"Yeah, from what I've seen before down there. I started out in that mine when it was nothing but a twenty foot tunnel. I've seen all the big veins. Not sure yet, but it does seem like it has some of the same strata we need."

"Keep at it. Anything else?"

"Payday."

"Oh, yeah, I forgot." Halverson took four envelopes from his side drawer and handed them to Leonard. "For the past week. Same thing next week. Remember, you find a good vein and there's a bonus for you—two hundred and fifty dollars in cash."

"Yeah, I remember. That's why we're working so damned hard." Leonard took the envelopes, put them in his shirt pocket, buttoned the flap, then waved and left the office.

Halverson thought again about Gwen. He looked down and saw that he'd lost it. Goddamn! If Gwen was still in a state. . . . He went out to her desk. No one else was in the office. The sweat had vanished from Gwen's upper lip, and the tinges of red were gone from her neck. She looked up, cool and in control.

"Yes, Mr. Halverson. Was there something you wanted?"

He lifted his brows, shook his head and went back to his office.

McCoy found the Schatzman Boarding House and signed on. The rate was five dollars a week. He would have paid more. The room wasn't bad; the bed was not much good at all but better than the floor. He paid for a week in advance, moved his carpetbag over from the hotel and decided it was time to find some lunch.

He stopped by the dress shop and motioned for Jessica to come out to the door. Ten minutes later they sat in the Ox-Bow Café eating what the natives there called lunch.

"Has your aunt told you anything else about the town, or why she and the others here seem so on edge, so afraid?"

"Not a word. Instead I'm learning to sew. It's exciting to take some cloth and needle and thread and making something I can wear."

After lunch she took him up the alley in back of the store, opened the back door and looked inside. It was a storeroom that was shut off from the main shop. Jessica grinned, caught his hand and urged him inside.

In the semi-darkness she leaned up to be kissed. He sensed the heat from her lips, and then her breasts touched his chest and she moaned softly. She kissed him hotly, her mouth opening and then closing. When the kiss ended she hugged him tightly and put her head on his shoulder.

"That is so delicious." She nibbled at his lips. "Spur, would you do me a favor? Only once it's happened and I kind of forget what it was like. Would you . . ." She caught his hand and placed it over her big breast. "Would you kind of . . . feel me a little?"

McCoy didn't move his hand. "Jessie, are you sure?"

"Yes! I'm just curious. You've felt lots of girls. It won't affect you, but I want to see how it feels. Please."

He kissed her cheek and let his hand begin to caress her breast. He found her hard nipple and tweaked it once, then again. She gasped and kissed him.

She undid two buttons and moved his hand under her blouse. He worked under her chemise until his hand touched her bare breast.

"Oh, Lord!" Jessie gasped. "Oh, that's . . . that's . . . I've never felt this way before, Spur McCoy. But I know you won't go any farther. I know you won't really do me all the way."

He fondled her breast, pinched her nipple and thought she would climax. She shuddered once and then stopped. He caught her hand and moved it down to his belt and the long bulge just below it.

"Oh my! I've . . . I've never felt it down there." She kissed him then, her mouth open, her breath coming in sucking gasps. Her tongue darted into his mouth and her hips began to push against his in a slow rhythm.

When her mouth came away she sighed. "Oh, damn, I wish it could be. I've never felt this hot before, all warm and melting and wanting something and not knowing quite what."

He pushed her blouse aside, lifted the chemise and kissed her breast. Her eyes went wide, and she gasped. He kissed her breast again and then licked her nipple.

He reached down and found her legs apart. His hand came to her crotch through the cloth of her skirt and massaged her dampness until she moaned. Then she clutched her hands around him and powered into a surging, humping moaning climax. It drilled through her once and almost stopped, then came again. His hand massaged her breast, and she finished the climax with a low squeal. She fell against him so he had to grab her before she dropped to the floor.

It took her several minutes to recover. When she did she leaned away from him.

Her eyes were wide, her mouth still open in wonder as she stared at him.

"That's what it's like every time? That's part of making love?"

"Yep, some of the best part. We better walk around to the front and let you get yourself pulled together." He buttoned her blouse and straightened it.

"One more kiss and a long hug," she said. After the kiss she stared at him. "You knew I'd never climaxed that way before, didn't you?"

"An easy guess. You're a virgin."

"Lordy, I don't feel like one now."

"You are, and don't forget it. And don't try that little petting trick on anybody else. If I'd been a young boy your age, he'd have had you on your back and your legs spread and been inside you in about two minutes. You wanted me to, I know, but I knew you really didn't mean it. You'd hate me tomorrow. Just take it easy. You're growing up fast enough as it is."

They were outside by then. She held his arm, her thigh touching his with each step.

"But the rest of it—the poking. What's it like?"

McCoy chuckled. "Jessie, you'll find out soon enough when you get married. Just be glad what we had there today and don't try it again. I won't let you again, you hear?"

"Yes sir, Mr. McCoy, sir." She grinned. "You know by now that I'm in love with you."

"That will pass. Just keep your blouse buttoned and your knees together."

She laughed. "My mother kept telling me that."

When they came to Main Street, she let go of his arm and walked beside him properly. He nodded at the door to the shop and moved on down the street.

Somewhere in this town was the key to the puzzle. Just what the hell happened to Colonel Potter? With this much fear, it had to mean that the colonel had been killed. But how and why, and most important, who did it? McCoy walked down the street, staring at everyone and wondering which one would crack and give him the information that he needed.

Chapter Six

The rest of the afternoon, Spur McCoy wandered the town. He knew when he and Jessica came out of the café that someone was following them. He saw the man again when he left the general store where he bought a new shirt and a brown leather vest.

It would be Halverson putting a man on him to check him out and be sure that he wasn't a robber or someone from the outside to steal away his whole town. McCoy let the man tail him. He had coffee in a café in the middle of the afternoon, then took a short walk down to the stream that ran a block from Main Street. He sat in the shade and threw rocks in the water.

McCoy knew he should be talking to people about this town, but he didn't know who to query and he

couldn't do it with the man tailing him. Neither could
Spur let the man know why he was there and delib-
erately ditch him.

He tried the barbershop and had his hair trimmed,
but the barber wasn't in a talkative mood, not even
when he told the tonsorial expert that he had just
signed on to work for Mr. Halverson. That comment
brought only a grunt and some quick snipping with
the scissors.

"Boy, about eighty percent of the people in town
work for Halverson one way or another. Me, for
instance. I rent this shop from him. If'n I make
enough to pay the rent, fine. If I don't he don't
care and makes me pay him anyway. Tarnation, can't
figure out how that man lives with himself. He's got
so much money now he don't know what to do with
it all."

That was the last thing the barber said before he
charged McCoy 20 cents for the haircut.

About five o'clock, he stopped by at the dress shop.
Jessie said she would be ready to leave at five-thirty.
Her aunt had agreed that they did owe him a home
cooked dinner to thank him for his gallantry in the
stage coach.

He stepped inside the dress shop and closed the
door. At least the tail couldn't hear what they were
saying. When he told her about the shadow on him,
Jessie frowned.

"Halverson is the richest man in town, so no matter
what happened here, it had to have had his approval.
Don't you agree?"

"Unless the richest woman in town wanted it to
happen, even though the richest man didn't want it

to happen. There could be a problem there. We'll probably never find out."

McCoy laughed softly. "Enough of that. What are we having for dinner?"

"Aunt Wilda never did say. She was considering fried chicken and ham. Hard telling what she'll come up with. She is proud of her good cooking, though, so I'm sure you won't be disappointed."

Jessica paused, looked at him and smiled in a secret way. "This noon in the back . . . that was just so thrilling to me. I've never felt anything like that in my whole eighteen years of life." She paused and looked at him. "Did I . . . I mean, was I pleasing to you?"

"Jessie, I wasn't exactly standing there like a pillar of granite. You felt my reaction. Just because I didn't throw you down and make furious love to you didn't mean that I didn't want to."

"Oh, good. I wondered."

"Little lady, have no doubts or confusions. You can arouse a man's sexual appetites as good as any female I've ever seen. Have no worries about that. What you need to be cautious about is just when to do that arousing. Remember, men are built with short fuses. We tend to go off in a rush. Sometimes just a smile from a pretty girl can get a man roaring with excitement."

She took two steps toward him.

"No, Jessica. This is a public place and someone could come in at any time."

"I just wanted to touch your hand."

When he held it out she gripped it, sighed and let go. "Maybe sometimes we could . . ." She looked up. "We could do that again. You know, not all the way, but just a little rubbing and touching."

"You're curious, right?"

"I keep thinking about it. Sometimes when I hear older women talk they are so frank that, I can't believe it. One woman back home told my mother that more than once she's had to clear off the kitchen table, strip off her clothes and do it with her husband right there on top of the table."

McCoy laughed. "Curiosity can be a fine thing. Just don't let it go too far. About doing that again, I'm not sure. That one time should keep you happy for a while."

"You never can tell," Jessie said and grinned.

They arrived at her aunt's house at six o'clock. The neat two-story house sat on a large lot with trees around it. He saw an apple tree in back that had ripening fruit.

Inside he caught the smell of cooking, but he couldn't identify it. Wilda met them in the hall.

"Mr. McCoy, I'm so glad you could come for supper. I'm not quite ready for you. Why don't you and Jess play some dominoes in the parlor."

"Mrs. Edwards, I'm delighted to come. A good home cooked meal for a man like me is a real treat. Dominoes? Yes, I think I can stand being trounced a time or two."

In the parlor they set up the game, turned over all of the tiles, then drew out seven each.

"You really want to play?" Jessica asked.

McCoy grinned. "We better. I have a double five."

They played for ten minutes until supper was ready. It began formal and proper, with McCoy complimenting Mrs. Edwards on how good the meal

was and she accepting the praise. They talked about
the weather and the economy in the town and the dim
prospects for the future without the mine.

McCoy grew restless. He put down a half-eaten
drumstick and looked sternly at his hostess.

"Mrs. Edwards, I must be frank with you. You have
a strange little town here. I arrive friendly and open,
and I find a town so closed and hostile that nobody
will talk to me even to tell me what time it is.

"Even you are controlled, cautious, careful, talking
only in generalities and on safe subjects. The only
person I can talk to normally is Jessica. That's because
she's a newcomer here, too, and doesn't know anything more about the town than I do.

"Mrs. Edwards, something is going on in this place
that isn't right, and I intend to find out what it is. I
need a small window to peek through. I want you to
be that window. Will you help me?"

"Young man, this is my town. I've lived here for
seven years now, and I don't have any idea what
you're talking about."

"Mrs. Edwards, I don't want to be unkind, but when
you spoke just now your hand was shaking and your
lower lip was quivering. You wouldn't look me in the
eye because you knew what you were saying was not
the truth." He looked at them seriously. "Can you both
keep a secret?"

Jessica nodded. He looked at Mrs. Edwards. She
frowned, closed her eyes and shook her head gently.

"Oh, Lord, I don't know what's going to happen
to us, to the whole town." She looked him straight in
the eye. "Yes, Spur McCoy, I can keep your secret.

I'll not breathe a word of anything that is said here tonight."

Spur grinned. "Great. I work for the United States Government as a Secret Service Agent. You may not have heard of us. We protect the currency, we handle federal law violators, and we help out cities and counties when they call on us for aid. I'm here to solve the disappearance of a man known as Colonel Amos Potter."

Wilda Edwards gasped, and her face went white. She leaned back in her chair with her hand to her chest.

"Oh, good Lord!" It was a cry of anguish and fear.

"Then you do know of him. You know that he arrived here in Timber Break."

Her face reclaimed a little color. A small frown spoiled her face, and she shook her head. "Young man, I didn't say that. I didn't say anything of the kind. I'm sorry, but I'm not feeling well. I think I'll go to my room and lie down for a while."

Mrs. Edwards rose from her chair, nodded at them and hurried out of the room.

McCoy sat there and frowned. He had hit a nerve, an extremely sensitive and raw nerve.

"She does know about the man, I can tell," Jessica said. "She's a strong lady, but the mention of that man's name brought an immediate reaction. She was nearly paralyzed with fear."

"What is she afraid of?" McCoy asked.

Supper was over. In the kitchen she washed, and he dried the dishes and put them in the cupboard. The rest of the chicken went into an icebox. It had a large chunk of river ice in the top of a box and shelves below to hold food where the cold air from the ice would sink to the bottom.

A half hour after Mrs. Edwards had hurried to her room, Jessica and McCoy sat in the parlor.

"I've never seen my aunt more terrified." Jessica said.

"I'd say that almost everyone in town is just as frightened as she is, which is making my job that much harder. All it takes is to find one person who will talk, but the problem is finding that right person who will talk and keeping him alive to testify."

"What on earth could make a whole town terrified?"

"Knowing something terrible that happened here. I've seen it once before. The agency is afraid that since he hasn't surfaced anywhere in nearly two months, Colonel Potter must be dead. Just how he died and who killed him is what I must discover. In this other small town two strangers were raped, tortured and then killed, and the whole town benefited. So the whole town was to blame, and they stuck together for a long time."

"I just hope the same thing hasn't happened here," Jessica said. "What could be so terrible that it could affect even my Aunt Wilda?"

"Potter must have died here. It might not be the death alone, but the threat that someone made along with it."

"Like if anybody talks about this killing, they will be dealt with in the same way?" Jessica asked.

"That certainly could be the reason behind the fear— knowledge of a dastardly killing, and a threat of death for anyone who violates the code of silence."

"Oh, dear, this seems like such a nice little town."

"It is. All it takes is one power or money hungry bastard to change a town like this into a boiling cauldron of hatred, fear and anger."

"The mine owner?"

"A woman owns the mine, I understand. The mine is worked out. What would she have to gain by a fear campaign like this one?"

"I don't know."

McCoy stood. "I better be going. Thank your aunt for me for the delicious dinner. Sorry I upset her so about the secret, but so far she's my best bet for finding out what's happened here."

"I'll try to get her to tell me something about it, like who the people are who are making threats against everyone."

They went to the door. She lifted up and kissed him gently on the lips. She caught his hand and pushed it towards her breasts, but he pulled away.

She frowned and kissed him again, a hot, hard kiss, that brought her mouth open.

He finished the embrace and stepped back.

"Now, Miss Edwards, I thank you for a fine evening. I think I should be moving along, and you can go and see if there's anything you can do for your aunt."

She frowned at him. "Yes, Mr. McCoy, I guess you're right. Come see me at the shop tomorrow and I'll take you out to lunch. Turnabout is fair play."

She touched his arm and he stepped out the door. McCoy thought about the woman's reaction when he had mentioned Colonel Potter. She had nearly collapsed. There was a terrible fear in her which he didn't know if he could ever overcome. Someone in town had done a masterful job of terrorizing the locals. He had to find out who it was, and exactly what happened to Colonel Potter.

Leonard Diederman picked up his brother-in-law about four that same afternoon. He met the other three men at the usual spot a half mile from the silver mine in a stand of small trees. The Silver Stake mine had been closed for over a year and had one guard on duty during the day and one at night.

The night man mostly sat in a small building outside the mine entrance, played solitaire, talked to his cat and nipped from his bottle of cheap wine. It was no problem getting past him and into the mine.

The five men walked from where they had left their horses in the grove. The mine itself was two miles outside of town so they had rode out to save time.

Leonard was a top shaft and tunnel man. He could lay out a system of tunnels, shafts and drifts that would saturate a given area of the mountain without letting it collapse. Most of the tunnels were exploratory, searching for the veins of the blue clay that held the silver.

For the past two months Leonard and his helpers had been scratching around the various tunnels of the Silver Stake, searching for what Leonard knew for sure was a continuation of the old vein. It had not petered out gradually but had simply shut off when it was two feet wide. Silver didn't do that. He figured there must have been some kind of an upthrust or volcanic activity that broke the vein and shifted that part of the mountain to one side.

It could have moved it a dozen feet or a dozen miles, but he had no way of knowing. Chances are it went only a few yards, one way or the other. Tunnel 12 had produced the most good ore, so he had concentrated on it the past two weeks.

"We gonna hit it tonight?" one of the men asked Leonard.

"Hell, I don't know. We'll find it if it's there, for damn sure. All we have to do is move a lot of rock and dirt and find that damn vein."

They worked four hours in the dim lights of the lanterns. They had no ventilation, no one to bring them cooling water, no relief. At the end of the four hour shift they had penetrated another six feet down the shaft. They had reduced the height of it to three feet so they wouldn't have to move so much worthless rock and dirt.

The men worked on their knees, digging out the rocks and dirt with a pick and shoveling the dirt into buckets while the other two men hauled the buckets out and emptied them. At least it wasn't hard rock here that had to be drilled and dynamited. They wouldn't have been able to get away with that without rousing even the half-drunk night guard. They had used wheel-barrows and dumped the waste rock and dirt down a shaft that went down to the third level below the second level they worked on.

At the end of the four hours they had found a handful of the blue clay, but not enough to get their spirits up. They dragged themselves out of the mine, slipped past the guard and walked the half mile back to their mounts where they had left their midnight meal. They carried thick sandwiches and fruit, and drank their fill from the chattering mountain stream that bounced on its way down towards the larger river below.

"Another damn wasted night," Trotter said. He was the crybaby in the group. "When in hell are we gonna find that vein?"

"Remember, old man Barton looked for it for two months and never found a trace," Leonard said. "We're just getting started. And don't forget that when we do find it, we each get a big cash bonus and then steady jobs as foremen when we get the mine open again. Steady wages at a good pay scale."

The men grumbled a bit more, finished their meal and then went by separate routes back to their homes in the sleeping town of Timber Break. No one had an inkling about what they did on their trips out each night. Their wives didn't even know, but when they brought their pay envelopes home, the wives didn't worry too much about what they were doing.

Chapter Seven

After the unproductive dinner at Mrs. Edward's, Spur McCoy went back to his boarding room and got to bed early. He put his Colt .45 on the bed near his pillow. There was a chance that Halverson had decided he didn't want Spur to work for him after all and would send a midnight caller.

The night passed without any visitors, and McCoy had breakfast in the morning, then started up the street to go to his new job for Halverson. He hoped the inside position might give him some clues to just how Halverson operated, and maybe at the same time he would hear some gossip about Colonel Potter.

He was almost at Halverson's when a carriage pulled alongside and the driver motioned him over.

"The lady in the carriage would like to have a word

with you, sir," the driver told him. McCoy took three steps to the closed carriage door and opened it. Inside he saw a strikingly beautiful woman with long blonde hair that fell almost to her waist and a dazzling smile highlighted by darting green eyes. She looked him over and grinned.

"So this is the newcomer in town who has been turning the ladies' heads. Get in, and let's take a short ride. We need to talk."

"You must be Cheyenne Barton, the town's richest person. I don't understand what we have to talk about."

"That's what makes it so interesting. You'll never find out standing out there."

"I'm on my way to an appointment."

"It can wait. Any appointment can wait." She smiled, and the effect was intoxicating. "I promise that you won't be bored. Really, what do you have to lose, Mr. McCoy?"

He shrugged. Halverson could wait a while. How else was he going to meet this lady? He stepped into the plush carriage, and the rig moved ahead.

"Spur McCoy, I am Cheyenne Barton. It's good to meet you." She held out her hand and he took it. There was no tingle or sexual tension, but he did feel something start to rush full of hot blood down around his crotch.

"I'm curious, Spur. What is a young, handsome, vigorous man like you doing here in Timber Break?"

"Trying to make a living. I was on my way to work for Mr. Halverson when you came by."

"Now, that's a laugh. Just what Halverson needs— a gunman. I understand that you have done good work with that six-gun on your hip. How would you like to be my bodyguard?"

"Why do you need a bodyguard, Miss Barton?"

"Please, call me Cheyenne. Why? From time to time I do get pestered. A bodyguard warns people away before they can get to the pestering stage."

By that time the rig had stopped. "We get out here, Spur. This is where I live."

She stepped down when the driver opened the door on her side. Spur went out behind her and closed the door. She said something to her driver, and he vanished into a shed in back of the three-story house. The driver returned a moment later in a light buggy with a fancy gray in the harness.

"I have a short trip to make. Spur and I want to use the buggy. Will you drive for me?"

McCoy nodded. The woman was more stunning standing than sitting in her coach. She was nearly six feet tall, built with generous hips and bosom and a tiny waist pinched in by a corset. Her green eyes watched him as he obviously admired her.

"Do I pass your examination? I hope so. Here, help me up."

A few minutes later they were on the stage road that ran down along the valley for several miles, tracking the creek that she called the Big Timber River.

Quickly they were into the country with all signs and sounds of the village left behind. The sun was up but not yet too warm. Drops of dew remained on the grass. Birds sang, and across the way on the other side of the stream, McCoy spotted a doe and her fawn near the water.

"Just what do we have to talk about?" McCoy asked.

"You don't enjoy the ride? I'd think that would be enough for most men. If that isn't, you're alone with me. Am I such bad company?"

"Not at all. My caution is that I've grown to be on my guard when a beautiful woman makes the first move to meet me. The odds are that she wants something or needs something from me. Is that why you asked me on this drive?"

Cheyenne laughed, and he enjoyed the sound. "Oh, heavens, no, Spur. If I want something I buy it. If I need something done, I hire someone to do it. I have plenty of money to take care of any and all of my wants."

"That must be nice. Since you're so well placed here in Timber Break, you must know just about everything that goes on in town."

"I do have some sources of information."

He turned and watched her. "Then tell me exactly what happened to Colonel Amos Potter when he came into Timber Break about two months ago and was never heard from again."

Her eyes flared for the briefest of moments, then returned to normal. "I'm afraid I don't keep track of those who come into town and those who go out. The stage line people keep records of tickets they sell. Perhaps they could help you. I like to know what's going on, but only in those areas that interest me."

"So you say you haven't heard of Colonel Amos Potter?"

"I'm afraid not, Spur. Sorry I can't help you. Oh,

here we are. Swing in right over there by the river. There's a ford there, and our destination is down there another fifty yards to that patch of trees. I want to show you something."

He turned in at the spot, went across the stream that was no more than a foot deep and about 15 feet wide and pulled to a stop under the shade of a canopy of hardwood trees that flanked a wide grassy place beside the stream.

McCoy tied the reins, stepped out of the rig and went around to help her down.

"Oh, there's a picnic basket and a blanket in back. Would you bring them. This is the best picnic spot in the county."

"We're here on a picnic?"

"When better to talk? We can relax in the wonders of nature, watch for hummingbirds and butterflies and enjoy the stream. This is one of my favorite spots."

"Then there's always the picnic. You planned this?"

"Of course, nothing happens without planning. Now spread out the blanket so we can sit down."

When the blanket was spread, they sat down, and in the process the hem of her skirt hiked up over a stocking-clad ankle. She didn't bother to push it down.

"Since it's too early for the picnic, let's talk, Spur McCoy. Where do you come from?"

"Here and there, down the trail, hither and yon."

She laughed. "Now that's the kind of man I appreciate. Would you like to kiss me, or did I misread the looks you've been giving me."

"No misread." He leaned toward her, she edged

closer, and their lips met. This time the sparks did
fly. McCoy jolted back and eyed her curiously.

"Were we struck by lightning?"

"I felt it to. We could try again." They kissed again,
and this time her mouth came open. She grabbed his
shoulders and pulled him down as she lay back on
the blanket. He was spread half over her body, and
his lips stayed on hers. Her tongue darted at his lips,
broke through and invaded his mouth.

When he pulled away he saw that her eyes were
closed. He kissed her lips and eyes and cheeks and
then her nose.

"Did you plan this part as well?" he asked.

"This part doesn't take planning. It either works or
it doesn't work." She reached up and unbuttoned the
fastener on his vest, then his new shirt and worked
her hands inside. He did the same to the buttons
on her blouse and found there was nothing under
it. Her breasts flowed against his hand. They were
warm already, and when he found her nipples, they
were hard and throbbing.

He pushed her blouse aside and kissed her breasts,
then licked her nipples and chewed on them as she
moaned softly under his caresses.

She gently moved him aside and sat up.

"I flatten out too much when I lay down. I want you
to see my sweethearts in all their natural glory." Her
breasts surged outward, with pink areolas and deeper
red nipples that quivered as she moved.

"You like them?"

"Beautiful. I'd like to chew them both down to
nothing."

She stroked his crotch, found his erection through

his pants and rubbed it. "Does he ever come out in the light of day?"

"Only if he's asked to."

She laughed and undid the buttons on his fly.

"Oh, glory! I knew he'd be big and thick. So wonderful. I could just kiss him!"

She bent and kissed his cock from the roots out to the purple tip.

She looked around. There wasn't a living soul for three miles in any direction.

"Are we alone?"

"Probably. No sense in taking any chances we don't have to, like undressing stark naked. Just take off the essentials."

She grinned, lifted up on her knees and worked under her long skirt. A moment later she sat down and pulled her silk bloomers off her feet.

McCoy kissed her again, then pushed her down gently on her back. Her legs spread apart, and he lifted her skirt around her waist.

"Damn, McCoy, hurry it along, will you? I'm about ready to explode!"

He went between her thighs and nudged forward. Her hands caught him and guided him, and a moment later he felt the soft, wet place and plunged in with one hard stroke until his pelvic bones ground into hers.

"Oh, God!" she bellowed. Her eyes went wild for a moment, and her face broke into a marvelous smile. "Now that is what I'd call a good poking."

"Hasn't even started yet," he said and stroked evenly for a minute. Then his hand found her hard node and twanged it.

"Damn, you know about doing that? Most men just

fuck off and are done. Oh, damn, but that feels good."
Her breathing jumped a dozen steps and sweat popped
out on her forehead. She gasped for air through her
mouth, and then when he felt he couldn't twang her
clit another stroke, she thundered into a climax.

She began with a long wailing cry, and then the
vibrations hit her and she shivered and shook in every
part of her body. The chant came next. "Oh yes, oh
yes, oh yes, oh yes!"

She shattered herself in one long series of involuntary spasms, rattling her body against him and the
blanket. She stopped, then gasped, and another series
ripped through her.

At last she shuddered, gave a long sigh and let her
arms fall to the side.

She lay there recuperating, and he slowly stroked
into her still feverish slot. By the fifth one she was
alive again and wrapped her legs around his torso,
tightening up her inner muscles and milking him every
time he pounded into her.

The pressure was fantastic. He knew he couldn't
stand it for long. He gritted his teeth to hold on for
more of the exquisite agony, but then she writhed her
hips against his in a circular motion and he exploded
without warning.

He grunted and bellowed and pounded hard into her
before he gave one last bray of accomplishment and
slowly sank down on top of her ravished body.

She wiggled at once. He moved to the side and let
her sit up. She ran her hands over his bare chest and
cradled his face in her hands, touching him as if he
were made of delicate china.

"A man is a wondrous thing," she said softly. He

barely heard her. Slowly his strength returned, and he sat up beside her.

He reached over and kissed her cheek. "Hey, that was amazing, terrific."

She kissed his lips lightly and smiled. "I was about to say the same thing. I don't know when I've felt so satisfied, so fulfilled, so really well-fucked."

They both laughed.

"We have our picnic and then we try to top it."

He put his hand on hers and shook his head. "Not a chance. There is no way that either one of us can be that good again. At least not for two or three hours. It was fantastic. Let's just let it stay that way."

She grinned. "Maybe I can change your mind by walking around naked for an hour or two."

McCoy laughed. "That could possibly do it, but suddenly I'm starved."

There were three kind of sandwiches, apples, peaches, local grapes and a pint of potato salad made the way he liked it with boiled eggs and onions and pickles. They had a giant jug of lemonade and half a cherry pie.

When the food was gone, McCoy lay back on the blanket and stared up through the green leaves at the patches of blue sky.

"Hey, this is the life—a great woman, a creek at your feet, the blue sky overhead and a fine meal. Wish to hell I had a cigar."

Cheyenne moved over beside him, lifted his head and put it on her lap. For a moment she giggled.

"What?" he asked.

"I was thinking that maybe later on I can talk you into turning over on your stomach and I could whip up my skirts real fast and you could chew on me down there a while."

"Tempting, but I always like to have a little nap after a good woman and a fine meal."

"Fine. I've heard that sex makes older men sleepy and young ones hungry."

"What do you mean by older men."

"Spur, darling, you're not sixteen anymore."

"Neither are you, darling Cheyenne."

She giggled. "I know. I'm too old to giggle, but I wanted to try a sixteen year-old a couple of years ago. I'd heard how boys fourteen to sixteen walk around most of the day with their whangers hard and ready to pop.

"I didn't tease him. I just told him I wanted to fuck him, and we ripped off our clothes and went at it. It's a record for me and I guess for him, too. Twelve times in two hours. Every ten minutes he was roaring to get into me again. Twelve times!"

McCoy groaned. "You're right. I'm not sixteen anymore." He sat up.

"You must know this town as well as anyone."

"I've been here for almost ten years."

"So what's the matter? The place is as tight as an old maid school teacher. Everyone is afraid and nobody except you and a newcomer has said six words to me since I arrived. They're so afraid they can't even talk straight."

She sighed and looked away. "I can't talk about it. Just don't ask any more questions. It doesn't concern you, so don't worry about it."

He reached out and touched her shoulder, then her cheek and followed down the curve of her face.

"I have to worry about it. I came here to find somebody who vanished, and I know he fell out of sight in this small town. Now I want you to tell me everything you know about Colonel Amos Potter. You do know about him, don't you, Cheyenne?"

"Oh, hell, no! Why did you have to ask me that? Judas, what can I do now? You're the best fuck I've had in years. Now you go and ask this."

"What's the problem? Have you heard of him? Is he here, or did he move on to another town? What happened to him?"

"I can't tell you."

"Can't, or won't?"

"Both. You don't understand. You could get hurt if I told you. Even I could get in big trouble. This is something you don't want to have any part of. Just forget it. Please forget it."

"I can't forget it. What happened to Colonel Amos Potter?"

She turned away. He caught her chin and turned her face back to him.

"He's dead, isn't he? That's why this town is so nervous, so afraid. Now tell me!"

Cheyenne jumped up. "What will you do? Shoot me if I don't tell you? Go ahead, shoot me. I'd be just as dead either way." She put her hand over her mouth. "Oh, damn!" Cheyenne ran for the buggy, stepped into it and tried to untie the reins.

McCoy got there before she had the leather free. He put his hand over hers, working on the reins.

"Hey, wait a minute. I'm sorry. I didn't mean to frighten you any more than you already are."

"You won't make me answer your questions?"

"Forget the questions. Forget I ever asked them."

"What time is it?"

He looked at his pocket watch. "Just about one o'clock."

She stepped down from the buggy. "Let's put the basket and blanket in the buggy and go for a walk. I feel like a nice long walk."

"A walk? Why not a buggy ride?"

"No, I want to feel the ground under my feet and stop and have a drink from the creek and then walk back. About five miles should do it."

"Five miles?"

She grinned. "That too tough a hike for you, city boy?"

The five mile hike proved long and tiresome, but uneventful. They got back to the buggy about three o'clock and drove back to her house.

When a man came to take the rig at the front of her house, they paused there a minute.

"I'm sorry I ruined the whole day with my questions."

She shrugged. "I've forgotten about them already." She paused. "Maybe you'd like to come to dinner some evening. My cook does a remarkable job."

"Maybe we can work out something," he said.

Cheyenne nodded. "I know what that means. I don't blame you. But the other part, before the talk, was just so wonderful."

"I'll get in touch with you," he said. She smiled, and he was sure she didn't believe him. Spur McCoy turned and walked back toward Main Street two blocks away and slightly downhill.

He heard the whispers as soon as he got to the

center of town. Groups of two or three talked on the corners and in front of stores. He walked down to the dress shop and went in.

Jessica looked up and smiled when she saw him, then motioned him toward the back. "Something terrible has happened. The whole town has been affected. If you thought people were frightened before, now everyone in the place has a bad case of the jitters."

Chapter Eight

Three hours before McCoy came back to Timber Break and while he was conveniently out of the way along the creek with Cheyenne, a strange procession walked down the center of town.

There were 20 hooded and robed figures, two of whom carried shotguns. The rest carried three inch thick black and red candles.

Ahead of them, with his hands tied behind his back, a small man stumbled along, looking from side to side and silently pleading for help. Once he cried out, only to be slugged from behind with a club that pounded into his kidney and silenced him after a gasp of agony.

The townspeople weren't sure what this would lead to, but they hung back, not asking questions. When the procession passed, half the town trailed the black robed figures down to the edge of the river.

The hooded figures stopped, and one of them tied the man's ankles together.

In the crowd a few whispered.

"Who is it?"

"The man tied up is Shorty Clawson, that old drunk. Somebody said he talked too much."

"What are they going to do?"

"Remember what they warned us they might do?"

"They wouldn't."

"They just might. Wish I had my rifle. I'd stop this in a hurry."

The two men looked at one another and shook their heads, then their attention went back to the man near the bank of the stream.

Not a word was said. The robed figures picked up rocks and all began throwing them at Shorty.

"For God's sakes, help me!" he bellowed. "These bastards are going to kill me. If you let that happen you're as guilty as they are. Come help me, you yellow bellies!"

A rock hit him in the stomach and he staggered backwards, but with his feet tied together he couldn't maintain his balance and fell over on his side.

The 20 figures moved closer. They used larger rocks now and one tore skin off his forehead. Another smashed into his chest and brought a scream of pain as a rib broke.

"Help me!" Shorty wailed.

The black robed and hooded figures moved closer. Now it was obvious that there were women in the robes as well as men. The women's throws were awkward, with little effect. Some of the men threw with force and accuracy.

Another rock jolted into Shorty's leg, and they could hear the bones break. Shorty screamed again, swearing at the robed figures, berating them as cowards.

"Come out from those damn black robes," Shorty brayed. "Let everyone in town know what a batch of murdering bastards you all are. I know some of you. Just to be sure everyone else knows I'm going to shout out your names."

The rocks came faster then. Two men moved within ten feet of Shorty and aimed one rock after another at his chest and head. One jagged stone smashed into his face, tearing his nose half off.

Shorty keened in agony, his voice high and sharp.

"I'm still saying the names. Jonas . . ."

A large rock hit Shorty's throat, smashing his windpipe and cutting off his words. He lay there groaning, writhing with pain.

After that the rocks came in a concentrated rain. One after another of the heavy stones slammed into Shorty's chest and head. A large rock hit him in the back of the head, cutting off all sounds from the small man.

The watchers shuddered, and many turned away. Before it ended half of them had hung their heads in shame and anger and hurried back to town.

At last the large man in the black robe and hood raised his hand and the stones stopped falling. Another figure went forward, touching Shorty's throat and looking for a pulse. There was none.

The undertaker's wagon creaked into view. The

undertaker picked up the body and loaded it in the wagon, then drove toward the cemetery.

There was no service.

The black robed and hooded figures marched back to town. There they vanished into buildings and stores and took off their robes and hid them away.

Clusters of people whispered on the street. In every store there were whispers of this wanton act of murder and cowardice.

Now, more than two hours after it all was over, the people still whispered about it.

Jessica looked up at Spur McCoy, and tears welled in her eyes and seeped down her cheeks.

"Where were you, McCoy? You could have stopped them. They marched Shorty Clawson through town and then stoned him to death. Where were you, McCoy?"

"Shorty Clawson, that harmless drunk I talked to yesterday? He couldn't hurt a fly."

"They said he talked too much about what happened here before. This was another warning to the people of Timber Break not to talk to strangers."

McCoy slammed his hand against the wall. "I was set up. Cheyenne Barton was giving me a tour of the river area. They wanted me out of town and they arranged it. Damn it to hell!"

"What can we do? This is murder."

"There probably was some kind of community murder before, probably Colonel Potter. That's the only thing I can think of that would make a whole town so paranoid and fearful. Now that fear has been reinforced a hundred times."

"The most important people in town must be in on

this," Jessica said. "That would include Halverson. And what about the mine owner, Mrs. Cheyenne Barton? I didn't see either of them among the townspeople. Maybe they were under the hoods."

McCoy's jaw tightened, and his face turned into a rock hard mask of anger. "I'm sure they both are involved. What I have to find out is how much they're guilty of. I know one good place to start." He jammed his black, low-crowned hat on and stormed out the front door of the dress shop.

McCoy marched down the street to the big three-story mansion where Cheyenne Barton lived. He went to the front door, twisted the mechanical doorbell and waited. After 20 seconds and no answer, he tried the door. It was not locked. He pushed it open and stomped inside.

"Cheyenne, where the hell are you? You've got some damn big questions to answer."

He saw a flash of a frightened Chinese girl's face, then it was gone. A few moments later Cheyenne came through a door into the parlor.

"Spur, so nice of you to come back quickly. You ready for another tumble in my featherbed?"

"Cheyenne, why did you meet me this morning and take me for that buggy ride down by the river?"

"Darling Spur, you must know the answer. I wanted to see your marvelous body naked. I wanted to be seduced by you. I wanted to make love in the grass and watch the clouds floating overhead. Didn't you enjoy our little outing?"

"I enjoyed it one hell of a lot more than Shorty Clawson enjoyed his march through town. You knew all about plans to stone Shorty to death, didn't you?

I was a problem, so you told the rest of them that you could get me out of town so I wouldn't interfere."

As he talked Cheyenne unbuttoned her blouse and pulled it off, walking toward him. She had her chemise removed before she got to him, and then she pushed her bare breasts against his chest and laced her hands around his neck.

He pushed her aside roughly.

"No! You've used your sexy body on me for the last time. What did Shorty do that was so terrible? Talk to me or some other stranger about how Colonel Potter was killed in this town?"

"Darling, don't be angry. I only want to make love to you and let you do anything you want to with me. I'll take you in all three holes as fast as you can get it up. You can fuck me while I stand on my head. All I want is your warm body against mine."

McCoy slapped her face.

Cheyenne smiled. "Oh, yes! Hit me, spank me. Make me bleed if you want to. I love it when you get rough with me. It makes me so hot I can't stand it." She wiggled out of her skirt and bloomers.

McCoy looked at her big, beautiful body and shook his head. "You murdering bitch! You and your friends are all going to pay for your little games. That's two killings, and I'd love to see you all hang. I don't know if Idaho has a territorial prison, but the whole lot of you are going to find out." He spun around and headed for the door.

The small Chinese girl he had seen before now stood between him and the front door. She was naked and held a small revolver in both hands aimed at his chest. Spur was sure she could fire it. Even a .32 round could kill a man.

He turned back to look at Cheyenne. One hand massaged her breasts, the other fingered at her crotch. She dropped to her knees then lay down, her legs spread, knees lifted.

"McCoy, come beat me and fuck me and make me happy again. You do a good job. I love the way you poke me."

McCoy snorted and turned back to the small Chinese girl. "Young lady, if you want to be in big trouble just hold that weapon about five seconds more and you'll be in prison or on a ship going back to China and slavery. You understand me?"

Slowly the girl lowered the gun.

"You want fuck-fuck me?" the small Chinese girl asked.

McCoy pushed her aside and stormed out the front door. Cheyenne knew about the stoning. She had set him up. She was in on it. Who else? Undoubtedly Halverson. A town this size couldn't pull off something like this without the town's owner being in on it. Hell, he probably organized it.

So McCoy knew he had to go see Halverson. He was supposed to start work for him today but Halverson certainly knew he would be late.

McCoy tried to get calmed down as he walked the three blocks to the Halverson offices. He went in, looked at Gwen and got off a halfway decent smile.

"Is he in? I was supposed to be here this morning."

"He's here, but he's with somebody. He said when you got here for you to wait. He wants to see you."

"Good, I want to see him, too." McCoy strode to the inner office door before Gwen could get off her chair. He jerked open the door and found Henderson talking to a man in miner's clothes, covered with dirt and spots of blue clay. Blue clay—prime silver ore. They must be finding something new in the old mine after all.

Halverson looked around, "Oh, McCoy, I'm almost through here. I want to talk to you."

"I want to talk to you, too, Halverson." McCoy saw two cabinets with closed doors. He walked over to them and pulled open the big doors.

"What in the world?" Halverson roared.

"I'm looking for your black robe and black hood, Halverson. You not only engineered the little rock throwing party today, you also maneuvered me out of town during the festivities. Didn't you think I'd want come to your little murder party?"

"McCoy, I don't know what you're talking about."

"Of course you don't. You'll probably say the same thing just before you drop through the trap door at your hanging." He opened the second cabinet but didn't find the robe. He moved toward the closet, but the miner now stood in front of it.

"Never mind, Leonard. Mr. McCoy, he was just leaving."

McCoy took three steps until he was in front of the miner. The man was nearly as tall as McCoy but not as muscular. McCoy looked back at Halverson, gave the appearance of relaxing, then turned and rammed his fist hard into the miner's stomach. Leonard gasped in surprise and pain and doubled over before he fell to the floor.

"Oh, sorry about that, Leonard. My fist just slipped." McCoy opened the closet door. The robe was not there.

"You must have put it somewhere else, Halverson. You got lucky today. It won't last. I'm giving you warning. I'm going to get you and your twenty partners in this pair of killings, and you'll wish to hell you'd never started all of this in the first place. Don't bother to get up. I know the way out."

McCoy was almost at the door with his back to the merchant, when he spun around, drew his Colt and put a round into the bookshelves behind Halverson.

The merchant had pulled a small handgun out of a drawer but hadn't aimed it yet.

"Don't ever shoot a man in the back, Halverson. There's no way to make it look like self-defense." McCoy cocked his Colt and centered the weapon on the frightened man's chest. "I could save the county a lot of trouble by gunning you down right here. Then again, I have this friend who is a hangman. Like to keep him busy."

McCoy watched Halverson sweat. Leonard tried to sit up from where he lay on the floor.

"He'll live for a while longer, Halverson. You're the one I'm worried about. I figure you might be the next victim to be stoned to death. Could happen, even if I have to throw all the stones myself. Think about it."

McCoy let the hammer down gently on the next round in the cylinder and left the room, backing out this time. Halverson never moved a muscle.

On the street, McCoy hurried over to the back door of the dress shop. He spoke to Mrs. Edwards, and as he watched her he knew she was about ready to fall to pieces.

"Mrs. Edwards, you know I'm a United States Secret Service agent, working for the government. I'm a federal lawman here to find out what happened to Colonel Potter. I think you know what happened. I heard about the stoning of Shorty Crawford. You know about that. Now I want you to tell me what happened to Colonel Potter. No harm will come to you, I promise. You must tell me so I can stop this killing."

Wilda Edwards sighed. She put down a dress she had been stitching and looked up, her eyes serious. She took a quick breath and nodded.

"I know. Maybe if I talked to you before, Shorty . . ."

"We can't undo that, Mrs. Edwards. Tell me what happened to Colonel Potter and who did it."

"Same group. The black robed and hooded cowards. They did it. They announced that it was for the good of the town. Said if Potter got away, all sorts of hell would rain down on the town and it could be wiped right off the map."

"So what did these robed killers do?"

"They said since Potter was a cruel man, he'd have to be treated with special care. They set a post in the ground in the middle of Main Street. Piled straw around it, then some brush and pitch pine and tied Potter to the post with wire. We thought it was some kind of a way to scare him. No one thought they would light the fire.

"He cursed them and called down the wrath of God on them. Then each of them struck a match and lit a torch. Then each threw his torch on the straw and brush at the base of the stake. They burned Colonel Potter at the stake!"

"My God!"

"They called everyone out in town to watch. Said we were all responsible. Said it was a cleansing of the town, and now we could get back to normal."

"When did that take place?"

"Along about two weeks before you came to town. They had captured the colonel and held him prisoner for a while. Guess they were trying to figure out what to do with him that wouldn't mean more trouble."

Jessica looked up with tears in her eyes. "That poor man. I can't imagine how people can do things like that. Then Shorty Clawson today!"

"It's terrible," McCoy said. "Once a sequence like this starts it's hard to stop it. That's my job—to stop it."

He told them about his confrontation with Halverson and how the merchant had denied nothing.

"So now they'll be trying to kill you," Jessica said. "You'll have to be extremely careful."

"Plan to. Might put in some time here in your back room if that's all right with the two of you. They wouldn't think to look for me here."

"It's not only all right—I insist," Mrs. Edwards said. "I'd have you at the house, but I don't want to endanger Jessie here. She's a real wonderful girl."

"Aunt Wilda, you're embarrassing me."

"Won't hurt you a bit, child. Now, you'll have to eat, Mr. McCoy. Jessica, you run over to the café and have Charlie fix me up a roast beef dinner and bring it back here. I have him do that from time to time. And bring a pot of coffee, too. Charlie won't think nothing of it."

"Mrs. Edwards, you really don't have to go to all of this trouble."

She smiled. "I know. That's what makes it all the more pleasurable for me. Jessica, you scoot."

Once Jessica was out the door, Mrs. Edwards walked to the back. "First thing we do is set up that cot I've been storing in here. Not perfect, but it'll work. I have some spare blankets and even a sheet or two. You can be comfortable here for a few nights. I do hope we can get this all settled before anyone else gets hurt."

"Mrs. Edwards, why did you decide to help me with this information?"

"About time somebody in this town had some backbone. Most of our men don't seem to have any. Now, after dark, you can go to your room at the boarding house and bring your belongings over here. Wouldn't trust those folks at that house far as I can poke them with a basting needle."

"Yes, Ma'am," McCoy said and grinned. He knew when he was outranked.

Chapter Nine

As soon as it was dark, Spur McCoy went through the back alleys to the boarding house, slipped out with his traveling bag without seeing anyone and went back to the dress shop.

That was when he made the connection. Leonard! That was the name of the man in Halverson's office that afternoon. Leonard was also the name of the man who had almost saved Winworth Barton the day he fell down the mine shaft. Cheyenne had told him the story that afternoon on their walk. Leonard Diderman had caught hold of Barton, but the mine owner had slipped out of Leonard's grasp. "Almost saved," came to mind again. Now he was working for Halverson, but Halverson didn't own the mine.

Then what was Leonard doing with what looked

like mine dirt on his pants and shirt and spots of blue clay that almost certainly could be silver bearing ore?

McCoy made his excuses to the ladies at the dress shop. "Something I need to check out. Oh, do you have a lantern?"

Mrs. Edwards did and handed it to him.

"You going to check the mine?" she asked.

McCoy grinned. "I hope I never have to try to keep any secrets from you. I don't know how long I'll be. I have a key to your back door. You two just go home and act normal, so you don't give me away."

Jessica watched him. "You be careful. We don't want anything to happen to you. A mine is a dangerous place."

He nodded and slipped out the back door. He had been told the day before where the Silver Stake Mine was situated, less than two miles from town. It would be quicker to jog out there than to go down to the livery and rent a horse. He checked his Colt on his hip and the extra rounds in his pocket, then he held the unlighted lantern in one hand so the kerosene wouldn't slosh so much and took off on a trot heading for the cliffs behind town and the silver mine.

He could see fresh horseshoe prints in the dust of the road even in the moonlight. Somebody was ahead of him.

He heard horses neighing about a half mile from the mine. Maybe it was Leonard looking into the mine. Was Halverson paying him to try to find a new vein of silver ore? At the entrance, he found the guard deep into a magazine, with a bottle of whiskey to keep him warm the rest of the night.

McCoy studied the guard shack. It sat near the main tunnel where the mine must have started. The tunnel had a heavy door on it that looked half-closed. A lantern inside the guard shack was the only light in the complex.

McCoy worked around the guard in the darkness, slipped inside the main tunnel and listened. He could hear nothing. He moved cautiously into the tunnel, then struck a match on the rock wall and lit his lantern.

First he checked the dust that must have collected on the floor of the tunnel over the year of idleness. McCoy found the center of the tunnel floor covered with boot marks and one wheel mark as if from a wheelbarrow.

He followed the footprints which went down the tunnel for about 200 feet. Then he came to a barrier and a shaft that dropped downward.

McCoy was not a tunnel rat and had little fondness for being underground, but this was a lead he had to check out. He found a wooden ladder on the side of the shaft, and by holding the lantern downward he could see that the shaft only went down 12 feet or so and vanished to the left in a new tunnel.

He went down the ladder, testing each rung. They were sure and solid. At the bottom, he found the boot tracks again. He shielded the lantern and stared into the tunnel but saw nothing. Far ahead he thought he heard metal clang on metal but he wasn't sure.

He walked down the tunnel slowly, came to a turn in the main tunnel and looked around it cautiously.

A rat scurried past him, and McCoy nearly dropped the lantern. He peered around the corner again and this time was sure he heard metal on metal. Far off he saw a glimmer of light. He turned the lantern down low and carried it behind him as he worked his way along the tunnel.

Every few feet he saw more of the boot prints in the dust and the wheel track. Now he could hear voices, some swearing, a laugh here and there, then a loud deep voice commanding someone to do something.

When he figured he was 200 feet from the workers, he turned out his lantern and shuffled along in the near darkness. The only guide he had was the increasingly strong light from at least three lanterns in front of him.

Fifty feet from the workers, he found an ore car on the tracks laid in the tunnel. He moved behind it, rested for a moment, then peered around the ore car.

Three men were working with picks and shovels. The mountain was comparatively soft at this point, with dirt and small rocks instead of granite and basalt.

Another 20 feet ahead he spotted a drift cut into the side. It could be only a few feet deep. It was another test tunnel to try to locate some ore. If he could get up there he could see what the miners were doing.

He waited until three of the men were working hard at the face of the tunnel, then he walked quickly to the drift and stepped inside. He put down his lantern, struck a match and carried it into the drift. It was 20 feet deep, eight feet high and six feet wide.

He went back to the main tunnel and listened to the men.

"Looks like the real thing to me," one man said.

"Yeah, but it might be only a foot thick bubble. Let's dig it out."

They worked with the picks again, and one of them yelped.

"Damn, that ain't no bubble! Frigger keeps getting bigger. Look at that vein of blue clay. Got to be two feet wide and getting bigger."

Now the fourth man came in view and studied the exposed part of the tunnel. When he turned in the light, McCoy saw that it was Leonard who recently had been crawling on Halverson's office floor trying to get his wind back.

"God damn!" Leonard said. "Gents, our work here is done. Fill up that bucket with the best of the blue clay and we'll knock off for tonight. Don't tell anybody about this, hear? A worked-out mine is cheaper to buy than one with a vein like this one. Come on, get that bucket filled and let's get moving. We've earned our money for tonight."

McCoy nodded. That explained one thing. Halverson wanted the Silver Stake Mine. He was probably furious that he didn't own it all from the start. All he got out of it was the price of the land sale to Barton. Now if he could get his hands on it, he could be a happy and extremely rich man.

McCoy figured Halverson would buy the mine or marry for it. He wondered why Cheyenne hadn't sold the property in the year since it closed. Maybe she kept it on Halverson's advice. That way nobody would buy it as long as he kept looking for more veins of the blue clay ore.

A few minutes later the four men came past McCoy with their lanterns. He was well back in the drift, and they passed quickly. McCoy lit his own lantern and waited at the mouth of the drift until their lanterns were out of sight around the bend in the tunnel.

A half hour later he had followed them out of the tunnel, slipped past the guard and took off for town.

He had heard the miner's horses head out for town just after he left the mine. Now he dropped his jog to a walk. He wouldn't be able to follow them, but he bet that Leonard would rush straight to Halverson's house with the bucket of rich silver ore.

As he walked back to town, McCoy wondered how he could use this information to his advantage. Dissention in the ranks? Yes.

When he reached town, he knocked on Cheyenne's big wooden door.

The Chinese girl opened the door, stood aside and waved him inside. A moment later Cheyenne came into the hallway.

"Well, you decided to come back for some more of Cheyenne."

"No, I came to tell you something. Halverson has had a four man crew working in your mine for some time. Tonight I followed them in and found them in a tunnel one level below the entry level.

"They brought out a bucket full of ore. They said it was a vein of rich silver ore two feet wide. Right now Halverson has the bucket of ore in his house, I'd bet. Why don't you pay him a visit and talk about it?"

She frowned. "I've known about someone in the mine now and then, but I didn't realize it was Halverson's men. That son of a bitch probably wants to buy the mine for a song." She marched up and down the hall frowning. "Why did you come and tell me?"

"I want to see you and Halverson in a big fight and blow apart this group you're both in. And I want to find out why Colonel Potter was burned at the stake. That's my price for telling you."

"I didn't agree to any payment."

"True, but you'll finally tell me, either now or later."

"Later. I want to get over and confront Halverson."

McCoy left the house and made his way back to the rear door of the dress shop. He used his key, slipped inside, then froze. A lamp lighted his cot. He saw a shadow move and drew his Colt.

"Spur McCoy, that you?"

"Jessica, don't surprise me that way. It could be dangerous."

She came around the stacks of boxes.

"You're back from the mine. Good."

He told her about the silver mine, the new ore, and Cheyenne's reaction to learning of Halverson's sneaky tactics.

"I want them to have a battle for the mine which has to be more important to both of them than covering up a killing."

She caught his hand and led him to the cot.

"What do you do now?"

"Worry about you."

"I told my aunt I wanted to talk with you. She smiled and said not to be gone too long. She knows that I . . . that I've fallen in love with you."

"You're eighteen."

"I'm a woman."

"I'm much older than you."

"That's the way it should be."

She kissed his lips gently, and he swore softly under his breath, feeling the attraction and knowing what just having her close did to him. He stood up.

"Little lady, you are a delicious package of woman. You are also a virgin and I aim to see you stay that way. I'm not about to get in trouble with your aunt. You just sashay your round little bottom right back to your house. No, on second thought I better walk you back there. No time for you to be out alone. Come on now, march. Time to go."

"What if I won't budge?"

"Easy, I pick you up, throw you over my shoulder and walk you home the hard way."

Jessica giggled. "All right. Seems strange having a man watching out for me. Ma and me were alone for such a long time. Let's go. I figure you got more important things to do with your time."

"Not more important than you, young lady, just different. Now, let's go. I do have some things to get done yet tonight."

After he walked her home and let her kiss his cheek, McCoy beat a straight line to Pris's house. She was home, the light was on, and she didn't have a customer. She grinned when he walked in the door.

"Heaven is smiling on me tonight. You here for business or pleasure?"

"Mostly business about your pleasure. I hear all sorts of things about this Friday night meeting they have in this town. What do you know about it?"

"The wild bunch. Yeah, I've heard. Whole bunch of them meet up at the big house that fancy lady Cheyenne owns. Been going on about three months. Nobody knows for sure who goes or what happens, but I got my suspicions. I think they play all sorts of sex games up there and just fuck up a storm."

"You talked to somebody who's been there?"

"No, just suspicions, but I can almost prove it. Up to three months ago I had me two more regulars than I got now. I mean these two bachelors hit me every week, rain or shine, they was here to get a poking. Ever since that Friday night jamboree, I ain't seen head nor asshole of either one of them.

"They are men who want their pussy regular. Neither one got married, and I did them a real service. Now they drop me like a syphillitic whore. Me, I figure that means one of two things. Either they got some poon on the side I ain't heard about, or they get themselves all fucked out up there on the big house's third floor every Friday night. That's where the lights all come from on a Friday night."

"Sounds convincing. What day is today?"

"Out of luck, cowboy. This is only Tuesday."

"More than one way to tip over an outhouse. Now don't give me that whore's code of honor shit. What I want from you are those two men's names, your former customers."

"Can't rightly do that, McCoy. You know that."

"Pris, two men died in this town. There could be half a dozen more. I'm here to stop this killing. If you want your town back the way it used to be and all your regular customers back, you better tell me before you get your tit in a wringer."

"You ain't shittin' me? You here like some kind of lawman to find out what happened to Colonel Potter?"

"That's the straight truth. Now tell me. It's important."

* * *

Ten minutes later, McCoy eyed a rundown house at the edge of town. Inside should be Yale Thornton, the town's watchmaker and repairman. One light showed through the front windows.

McCoy pounded on the front door and waited. A minute later the door opened a crack.

"Yeah, who is it?"

"A friend, Yale. Need to talk to you."

"Don't recognize you—"

McCoy slammed the door open, spinning the slender man backwards into the living room. He held a book in one hand and had a *pince-nez* perched on his thin nose. He jumped back a step, alarm clouding his face.

"If it's money you're after, I don't have any here." He looked closer. "Oh, it's you, that stranger in town who's prying around and asking questions."

"Right, Yale, little friend. You're just the man to do some answering. First, let me do some searching. Shouldn't be hard to find."

McCoy turned to the small closet near the front door. It wasn't there. He looked in the bedroom with Yale trailing behind him.

"I really must protest. I'm going to the sheriff tomorrow and file a complaint against you for breaking and entering, for searching my house, for . . ."

He stopped the moment McCoy pulled a black robe and hood from the closet.

"Now, Yale Thornton, I think it's time you and I sat down and had a long talk. I want to know the names of the other twenty people in your little Friday night sex party and committee to burn people at the stake and stone people to death. Where shall we start?"

They went back in the living room, and McCoy threw the black robe and hood on the couch.

"Now, Yale, I guarantee you that I won't breathe a word to anyone that I've talked with you. No one will know but you and me. If they found out you talked to me, you'd be the next one to be stoned to death, right?"

The slender man with the high forehead and nervous hands nodded.

"Today I didn't throw a stone that hit Shorty. I swear. I missed him everytime on purpose."

"I believe you, Yale, I believe you. Now tell me what happens on Friday night up at Cheyenne's mansion."

Ten minutes later the story of the sex parties had been fully told to McCoy.

"So, how did this little sex game turn into burning a man at the stake?"

"I really don't know. It just happened. One day we all got together and the problem was presented and we took a vote. It was twelve to nine to burn him. I . . . I was one who voted against the idea."

"Figures. Now, who is the kingpin? Who gives the orders and tells you what to do? Is it Cheyenne?"

Yale shook his head. "Oh, no, she was as surprised as the rest of us when this burning at the stake came up, but by then it was too late to back down."

"So who gives the orders?" McCoy asked.

Yale Thornton paced the small living room and shook his head. "Don't know if I can tell you."

"Then I'll have to spread the word tomorrow that you told me everything. How long do you think you'd live after that?"

"Oh, damn, I knew this whole thing was trouble.

But I got so damn tired of Pris every Wednesday night. Hell, I might as well tell you."

Something tapped at the front window. Yale turned toward the sound, a frown clouding his face.

The gunshots came at once.

Chapter Ten

At the first rifle shot, McCoy dove for the floor behind the sofa. He felt the additional rifle slugs hit the sofa and saw them shatter the plaster on the wall. He was about to move when the shotgun went off again.

McCoy lay there for two minutes listening. He had out his six-gun by this time but there was no target. The assassins must have figured they killed him.

He squirmed around the sofa. The lamp still burned brightly.

"Thornton, you all right?"

No answer.

He worked his way further around the sofa and there found Yale Thornton. He had two rifle slugs in his body, one in his head slightly below his left eye and the second in his chest.

Thornton apparently had been the target, not McCoy. Or had they wanted both of them but took out Thornton first?

At least he had a little bit of information. He knew about the sex games at the big house on Friday nights. They degenerated into this secret society that burned people at the stake and then stoned anyone who talked about it. Now they also murdered one of their own who was about to tell all.

McCoy left the light burning in the living room. He went out a sagging back door on his belly, making no noise whatsoever and ready with his Colt if anyone waited there for him. No one did.

Five minutes later he was back on Main Street. McCoy took stock quickly. Things finally were starting to move. He figured that Cheyenne and Halverson would have a big fight, and that tomorrow Cheyenne would have a crew in the mine checking out the find. Soon the mine should reopen.

All this would strain any cooperation between Halverson and Cheyenne. McCoy had half the information about the sex club. All he needed were more names, especially who dictated the death of Colonel Potter.

How did they know that Thornton was about ready to tell all to a stranger? Had they suspected him? Had his place been staked out by the group? Maybe they had followed McCoy from the whorehouse. If they did that, why not just kill McCoy then and get it over with? Would they know about the second man whose name Pris had given him?

There was no choice. He had to track down the

second man, Fred Oberholtzer, who had a house on the other side of town. He shared the place with his brother-in-law and sister.

McCoy found the house, saw lights on in both sides and knocked. No one came. He knocked again. Still no reaction. He heard someone sobbing inside.

McCoy tried the doorknob and pushed the door open. Through a foot wide slot he could see part of a kitchen and a living room beyond. A man lay on a small couch, his arm drooping down toward the floor. The hand held an empty whiskey bottle.

McCoy slipped inside, closed and locked the door, then walked over to the man on the couch. He was drunk but not passed out.

McCoy took the empty bottle and shook the man until his eyes opened. He stared at McCoy without understanding.

"Who . . . who the hell are you?"

"A friend. Heard you needed a shoulder to cry on. What the hell's the matter?"

"Don't you know? Man died today. Shorty. Knew Shorty. Nice little guy. We used to drink together sometimes."

McCoy knelt beside the couch and stared hard at the man.

"Are you Fred Oberholtzer?"

"Yeah, guess I got to admit it." He sniffled, wiped his eyes with the dirty sleeve of his shirt and groaned. "Why the hell did it happen? I didn't want it to. I voted no. Damn it to hell, I voted no, but I had to go along."

"You threw some of the stones?"

Fred looked up and nodded. "What the fuck? Of

course. If you belong to a group the majority rules, you go along. Still I didn't have to hit him with any of them. Damn it, why couldn't I just have said no?"

"Because then you would have been the next one stoned."

"Oh, yeah, we got that signal plain and clear. They made that easy to understand. Some of the women were so scared they pissed in their skirts, right there in the meeting before we marched down Main Street. Good thing they had them long black robes on."

Fred shook his head and tears came to his eyes.

"Goddamn it to hell!"

"You could always quit the group and ride out of town. They wouldn't come after you."

He sat up scowling. "Now why would I want to do that?"

"Get even with them. Hurt them. Get back at them for killing Shorty Clawson today. Wouldn't you like to do that?"

He stopped sniffling and looked at McCoy. "So who are you? Why are you interested?"

"I'm here to find out why Colonel Potter was burned at the stake, who did it and see a little justice done."

"Holy shit! I struck one of those matches. We all did. I guess we're all guilty."

"I want the ring leaders. Who is the top dog in this murder society?"

"I can't tell you that. They'd kill me for sure, then. Just can't". He tipped the bottle and drank. McCoy grabbed the bottle, but he was too late.

"Can't tell you," Fred Oberholtzer said. Then he let go of the bottle, his head rolled to the side and he was unconscious.

"Whipped again by demon rum," McCoy said. He stared at the man for a few moments. Nothing would bring him out of this for five or six hours. He'd try again tomorrow. Pris had told him that Oberholtzer managed the hardware and building materials store which Halverson owned. McCoy would stop by there tomorrow.

He couldn't think of anything else he could do tonight. He wished he could have confronted the men who shot down Yale Thornton. There must have been two of them. No man carries both a rifle and a shotgun.

He blew out the lamp, then went out the front door. He paused letting his eyes adjust to the darkness. He couldn't see anybody lying in wait for him. If there were, they would have blasted him with the shotgun by now.

McCoy edged along the wall of the house, walked to the street and down to the alley. A short time later he turned the key in the lock to the back door of the dress shop and went inside. All was dark and silent.

He struck a match, found a lamp and lit it. He hoped that Jessica wasn't naked in his bed waiting for him. She wasn't.

McCoy needed some sleep. It had been quite a day. This affair was winding up faster than he expected. The silver ore strike had been the capper. It would blow the two town leaders apart.

He had found out about the burning at the stake

and the stoning of Shorty and just how the sex games worked on Friday nights.

He still needed to know who the ring leaders were in the burning of Colonel Potter—who they were and why they did it.

McCoy settled down on the cot and blew out the coal oil lamp, but he didn't sleep for some time. He kept thinking about Jessica, but he knew he had to keep his hands off her. It was for her own good. He kept telling himself that until he almost believed it.

In the morning he left the dress shop before either of the women arrived, had breakfast and was determined to have a long talk with Cheyenne and extract his price for telling her about her new silver mine strike.

In the second largest house in town, Ludwig Halverson was busy fixing his wife's breakfast. Today had to be the day. Too much had happened too quickly. Somehow Cheyenne had found out about his men in the mine and the glorious discovery. He had denied anything of the sort. Told her last night that he had no idea what she was talking about. Why would he send men to dig in a mine he didn't even own?

Today she was bound to send some men into the mine to check. Today his wife had to die. He had been increasing the powder every day. His wife was bedfast now, and no one would be suspicious if she died after a long illness.

They had no doctor in town. The closest one was 30 miles down the road. Their doctor had died shortly after the mine closed, and they hadn't been able to get a new one to come to a dying town.

He spooned a full teaspoon of the powder into the cooked oatmeal and mixed it in thoroughly. Then he added brown sugar and lots of milk to disguise the taste. He guessed that she couldn't taste anything anyway by now but he had to be sure. This time he must be positive.

In an hour it should be all over. He would give her breakfast, then rush down to the office and send someone home to check on her as he usually did during the morning.

Maybe he would have Gwen check on her today. He hummed a soft little tune as he took the bowl of arsenic-laced oatmeal into his wife's bedroom.

She eyed him from her pillow.

"I'm not hungry," she said when she saw the oatmeal.

"Nonsense. How can you get well if you don't eat so you can stay strong? Come on now, I'll help. I have your tea and milk and some hot oatmeal with brown sugar, just the way you like it."

She still didn't want to eat. He fed her, spooning the oatmeal into her mouth until the last of it had been eaten. That made him feel better.

He gave her a drink of milk, then cleared away the tray. He took it to the kitchen and washed the oatmeal dish thoroughly. He removed the package of arsenic from the kitchen and buried it in the backyard where the soil had been dug up recently.

Back inside Hamilton noticed his wife seemed to be having difficulty breathing.

"I have to hurry down to the office, Ruth. You be careful. I'll send somebody around in a couple of hours to sit with you. I still think we should have some full-time nursing for you, but if you don't think so, I'll go along."

He looked at her. She moved her eyes and stared at him in desperation, he thought. He wasn't sure she could move her head. It wouldn't be long.

Halverson walked quickly from the house and downtown to his office. By noon it would all be over. By noon he would be free to woo and win Cheyenne so they could combine their fortunes. He was sure she would understand the business aspect of such a marriage. He could certainly understand her body. The taste of it he'd had last Friday had been intoxicating, even if she was high on her white tiger. He'd break her of that. Lud Halverson sat behind his desk and smiled. It wouldn't be long now.

Spur McCoy walked up to the big house on the rise and knocked on the door. The small Chinese girl answered the door. This time she bellowed something, left the door open for him and scurried away.

Cheyenne came from the kitchen. She wore a long thin nightgown that tied in front but still showed most of her great figure.

"McCoy, how thoughtful of you. You've come to breakfast. Ordinarily I'd try to get your pants off, but this morning I'm so busy my head hurts. I've contacted my three most loyal workers from the old mine crew and we're going into the tunnel in about an hour to find out if what you said was true.

"Halverson, that peckerhead, denied everything.

Said he never sent any men into the mine. Said the whole idea of finding a new vein of silver was wishful thinking. I just hope that you are right."

"I'm right. I saw it all. Now I want my pay. Why was Colonel Potter burned at the stake?"

She glared at him a moment, then shrugged. "I don't know why, but since I believe you about the mine, I'm honor bound to pay off. Colonel Potter was a brash, boastful, stuck-up little bastard. He came in here claiming to be a retired general, and he wanted to find somebody.

"The whole town knew the secret, but we weren't telling the little shit anything. He grew insistent and tried to throw some weight around. Shot at one of our men he thought knew something about the girl he came to find.

"Your Colonel Potter came here hunting Eloise Mae, the darling daughter of our glorious president in Washington D.C. Eloise Mae was an illegitimate daughter who the president had kept hidden. His political opponents found out about her and were ready to use it against him if he tried to run for reelection.

"Yes, she was here in town. Over the years she had felt abandoned and neglected. She ran away from home in Washington and during a five year stretch became lost to the president and his family. During that time she supported herself by selling her favors. By the time she got to Timber Break she was badly used, not pretty or young anymore but still able to sell her pussy for three dollars a whang.

"What the men didn't know was that she had syphilis, and in two months she infected six men here in town. One of the men was Jerry Halverson, son of our glorious city leader and owner of eighty percent of the town.

"He was outraged. Jerry knew he was sick and ran away to get some treatment. Two of the men infected are still in town and still sick. A third one shot himself, and the other two moved on down the trail.

"A week after Jerry left, Lud Halverson shot Eloise Mae dead and they secretly buried her at night. A week later a man came through town looking for Eloise Mae. He was a government man, had the girl's picture and confided to Halverson that she was the illegitimate daughter of the president. The nation's leader desperately wanted to find her.

"Halverson made up a story that she had been here for a time as a seamstress but left for Boise after a week's stay. Now Halverson was shitting purple. He knew if the president found out about his daughter being killed here in Timber Break that he would go to prison and the whole town might be burned to the ground and wiped off the face of the earth. He swore that would never happen."

McCoy nodded. It all rang true. No wonder the president didn't tell anyone what Colonel Potter's mission was.

"Now, to get this all cleared up, who is the leader of the hooded criminals who burned Potter and stoned Shorty Clawson?"

Cheyenne shook her head and opened her robe to show him her two large, perfect breasts.

"Hey, I agreed to tell you why Colonel Potter got himself burned at the stake—mostly because he was an asshole. I didn't agree to tell you anything else. Now, have you had breakfast or do you want a stack of hotcakes?"

Chapter Eleven

Never one to pass up a free meal, McCoy ate three of the best hotcakes and maple syrup he'd had in years, along with three strips of bacon and a big mug of coffee. Cheyenne's cook brought in more hot cakes but McCoy knew his limit. He thanked Cheyenne, kissed her breasts once and hurried out of the front door.

He had just made it downtown when somebody came racing out of Halverson's office with a black arm band on.

"Mrs. Halverson has died," he told everyone he met on the way to the undertaker. McCoy scratched his head. Now how did this fit in with everything that had happened? Or did it? He'd heard that Halverson's wife had been ill for some time.

He watched as Cheyenne met three men in front of a saloon and rode off toward the mine. Soon all hell would break loose over Halverson digging in her mine.

McCoy figured that Halverson, or whoever shot down Thornton last night and was probably now gunning for him as well, must be too busy this morning for such a small problem. To be on the safe side, McCoy used the alley and slipped into the back door of the dress shop to check in with the ladies.

"Everything's fine," McCoy told the two of them. "I found out why Colonel Potter was here and who he was hunting."

"Was it about that young whore who came to town maybe six months ago or so and then left after some of our men caught some wild French disease?"

"That was the one," McCoy said. "So we're starting to bring things together. Oh, you don't know about the huge new silver strike out at the mine. Word should leak out today sometime. I expect that the mine will open as soon as they can get it put back in shape."

"Glory be, then Timber Break won't die out as a town after all," Mrs. Edwards said. "I was starting to worry. My business has been cut in half in the past year."

"Should be picking up just fine in a month or so."

Mrs. Edwards smiled. "Good, then I'm going to go out and have a cup of coffee and a piece of pie over at Charlie's like I used to when we had some money."

She smiled at Jessica. "Girl, you watch the place while I'm gone. I'll be a half hour or so, or maybe more if I can get Charlie to talking. We used to talk all the time."

She put on a little hat, primped her hair and made sure her dress was all straight and proper. Then she walked out the front door.

"Aunt Wilda is sweet on Charlie," Jessie said. "She told me the only way a widow can get a man is to go out and make a real effort to interest one. That's what she's doing."

No customers were in the shop, so Jessica motioned him to the back where they could see the front door but not be seen.

She put her arms around Spur and pushed up close to him, resting her head on his shoulder.

"I've been talking to Aunt Wilda, you know, telling her about all these new wild feelings I'm having, how I find myself looking at men's crotches to see if they bulge or not, and wondering what's inside."

Spur grinned. "What did Aunt Wilda say about that?"

"She says she remembers how it was when she was about my age. No man had ever touched her. She was so curious she could explode."

"You feel the same way, right?"

"Yes. What would it hurt, just once? Aunt Wilda winked at me just as she left. She wouldn't be cross with you if you wanted to put it inside me—you know, fuck." Jessie grinned and blushed for saying such a naughty word. Then as she unbuttoned the top two fasteners on her blouse, Spur caught her hands.

"I thought we talked about this already. You found out about having a climax, remember?"

"Uh huh. But Aunt Wilda says a finger job isn't like it is when a man's deep inside you, plunging away like crazy."

"Jessie, you shouldn't be talking that way."

"Will you let me kiss you a little and just pretend?"

Spur didn't answer, and she kissed him hard. Her mouth came open and she pushed against him, grinding her hips against his, holding the kiss a long time. When she ended it, she sighed.

"Oh, I just feel so good." She caught one of his hands and put it over her breast. "Sweet Spur, we can just fool around a little, you know, like we did the last time."

"You little devil. You know what this is doing to me?"

"Making your big whanger hard and stiff?"

McCoy laughed. "The way you talk."

"Am I right? Is he all stiff?"

"Jessica, can't you wait just a while longer. Some man will knock you off your feet and—"

"I don't want to get married to the first yahoo who asks me just so I can find out about having sex. My mom did that and regretted it for twenty years."

She kissed him again, and his hand rubbed against her breasts, then worked inside and under her chemise to her bare skin.

She gasped, and her hips humped against him. Then she dropped to her knees and, before he could more than mildly protest, unbuttoned two fasteners on his fly.

"I want to see him. Don't deny me that. Just a crumb, just a little bit. It can't hurt a thing. I feel safe with you, Spur McCoy. This is why Aunt Wilda went to see Charlie. She told me to do it this way."

A moment later she had his fly open. She fished inside, then looked up at him. McCoy undid his gun belt and laid it aside. Next he opened his pants belt and let his trousers drop to the floor. He pulled down his short underwear and let his whanger rise up, stiff and ready.

"Oh, my, but he's so big. My finger will go in my little cunnie but never anything that huge." She looked up. "Can I touch him?" Spur nodded. She stroked him, touched his tight scrotum and fondled each of his balls. She looked up and nodded.

"Oh, I see, yes. I'd heard a girl talk about these." She went back to his penis and kissed the purple tip.

"Oh, my! He's so beautiful. I never expected anything so perfect, so like an arrow with a pointed head." She frowned for a moment. "I guess that's so he can push into my little cunnie easier, right?"

"Right," McCoy said. He bent and pulled up his shorts. Just before they covered him, she hurried and kissed he the tip once more, and his penis gave an involuntary jerk. She grinned.

"I think your big whanger likes me. Maybe one of these nights . . ."

"Probably not, little lady. Your education is almost complete. It's gone about as far as it can without getting into areas we shouldn't."

"Oh, lordy, I'm so hot! I feel like I'm burning up. I want you so badly." With one hand she rubbed her breasts. "Is it always this way?"

"It should be. Now you cool yourself down, young lady." He pulled up his pants, buttoned them and fixed his pants belt and then his gun belt in place.

Jessie looked at him. "Oh, no, looks like you want to leave. Don't leave or I'll die." She cupped both breasts with her hands. "Will you kiss them both for me before you leave? You did that other time. It felt wonderful."

She pushed inside her blouse and lifted her chemise. Her breasts popped out, large and perfect with hard nipples.

Spur bent and kissed them both, then nibbled at her nipples until she shivered and thundered into a climax. She pulled him tightly against her breasts as she tore through the climax. She wailed and moaned, her hips pounding forward against him as she pushed a breast into his mouth.

She came down slowly from her high, a glorious smile on her face.

"Oh, yes, yes, yes. That was pure heaven, Spur McCoy. What in the world could be better? How could it be better if your big whanger was poking inside of me? I don't know but I want to find out."

He pulled her chemise back in place and buttoned her blouse.

"Sweet young Jessie, you'll find out sometime. Just take what you have so far and cherish it. Then start looking for the young man you want to share your lovely body with for the rest of your life. Marriage and sex are both serious affairs. That's why they put them together.

"Now you be good, and take care of the shop. Your color will return to normal in five minutes. Maybe you won't have a customer before then."

He kissed her mouth gently, eased away from her, walked with determination to the back door, opened it, waved and vanished outside.

He had to get to the hardware store and have one more talk with Fred Oberholtzer. He had learned that the man had little to keep him in town, no wife, no lover, just his job at the hardware store. If what McCoy wanted to do would work, Fred might take a sudden trip to visit his relatives in Boise.

Without warning, a revolver belched flame and hot lead on the boardwalk 30 feet in front of McCoy. When the poorly aimed round sliced past his right shoulder, McCoy darted into the Henderson Real Estate and Land Office where a sturdy door frame protected him.

His own revolver came out of leather in a fraction of a second as he picked out the shooter, Leonard Diderman.

Leonard jolted into the street and hid behind a moving wagon half-filled with shelled corn, ducking low and moving away from McCoy who stormed after him. Leonard saw him coming and ran ahead of the team of horses, then angled away from McCoy trying to keep the bulk of the two draft horses between them.

McCoy snapped off a shot at the running figure. That brought a glance over Leonard's shoulder and another spurt of energy that carried him between buildings on Main Street and toward the alley in back.

Spur sprinted for the edge of the building, checked around it and ran to the back of the store. There he found a mass of trashed boxes, some wooden, some cardboard, and five 50 gallon steel drums.

McCoy would have to check the hiding places, but where to start? Let Leonard play the next card. McCoy stepped out from the corner of the building in plain sight, paused a second, then lunged back behind the wooden structure.

A revolver round barked into the high Idaho summer air, and the hot lead gouged a chunk of wood out of the side of the building. McCoy looked around and saw the puff of white smoke rising from behind a cardboard box 20 feet away. He reached around and put two slugs through the side of it waist high.

A scream of pain filled the alley for a moment. "Bastard!" Leonard shouted. The box moved a bit, and McCoy tried to guess its route.

Down the alley another 30 feet a horse stamped in the morning sunshine. It was saddled, ready to ride. McCoy wondered if Leonard had left it there as a getaway mount.

McCoy darted to one of the steel barrels and crouched behind it. He took no fire. He peered around the barrel and saw the big wooden box move slightly as if someone had pushed it or stepped inside.

McCoy flipped open his Colt, pushed out the two spent rounds and put in three fresh loads, giving him all six cylinders loaded.

He eased the hammer down on the loaded round and waited. He saw the problem before he could warn her. A schoolgirl, maybe 15, came between buildings to the alley, cutting through to her home probably.

"Go back!" McCoy shouted. She turned and looked at him. A second later Leonard leaped from the wooden box, caught the girl around the waist and held her in front of him.

"Now, McCoy, drop your gun or this young one is dead in a second."

"Not a chance, Leonard. You kill her and I put three rounds in you before you can pull the trigger again. You won't hurt her, because then I won't just kill you, I'll make you suffer. First I'll shoot your balls off, then smash a kneecap before I put another round through your shoulder joint. You'll be begging me to kill you."

"Bastard!" Leonard bellowed. He let the girl go and ducked behind the wooden box. Before McCoy could move, Leonard sprinted for the horse 30 feet behind him. McCoy snapped a shot at the running figure, then raced in the same direction.

Leonard mounted, whirled around the animal, leaned next to its neck and galloped straight for McCoy.

McCoy stood tall and straight, extended his Colt at arm's length and took careful aim. He fired while the charging bay was 20 feet away. The heavy .45 slug hit the horse between the eyes, and she went down in two seconds.

Leonard leaped off the horse and hit the alley running. He darted into a back door of a business and vanished. There was no sign on the door, so McCoy had no idea what kind of a store it was.

When he jiggled the door handle, two shots splintered through the thin door. McCoy screeched as if in pain, turned the knob again and let the door swing outward.

Leonard didn't take the bait. McCoy heard a woman scream inside the store, and he bolted through the opening and dove to the floor. The rear storage room was dark, with only light from the back door and one high window. He saw stacks of roofing, pipe and some cement blocks. He was in the hardware store, Fred Oberholtzer's place.

He had heard nothing more from the front of the store. McCoy moved down an aisle slowly, not making a sound. He came to a curtain that closed off the back from the front. He took a shovel handle and pushed the curtain while he stood to the side. Two shots snarled from the front of the building and the lead zapped through the curtain, making it dance.

McCoy dropped to his knees and looked under the curtain where it cleared the floor. He could see the front of the store. Leonard held a woman with one arm across her breasts and the six-gun leveled over her shoulder.

To the side he could see Oberholtzer standing in surprise and fear.

McCoy brought up his Colt and edged the muzzle to the bottom of the curtain. He held the weapon sideways so he could get the right angle and waited. The woman fainted and sagged forward, exposing Leonard's chest. McCoy fired. He came to his feet and charged forward through the curtain, ripping it down.

Ahead, Leonard had dropped the woman and ran for the front door, his left hand covering a bloody spot on his chest. He rushed out the door before McCoy could get off another good shot and vanished into the throng of people on the boardwalk.

McCoy heard a scream ahead of him and saw a woman jump back. He rushed that way and saw Leonard sagging, his left hand holding the gun now, his right hand hanging at his side, blood running off his fingertips.

Leonard turned and lifted the six-gun. The people on the boardwalk scurried out of the line of fire, and McCoy lifted his Colt and triggered one more round which slammed into a rib over Leonard's heart, killing him.

A man kicked the six-gun away from Leonard's dead hand. Two women peered at the corpse, then backed off chattering about the small drama they had witnessed.

A man ran up. He had a silver star on his chest that read Sheriff. He looked at McCoy as he walked up to the body.

"You shoot Leonard?"

"Self-defense, Sheriff. He had his six-gun trained on me. Ask anyone."

The man who kicked the gun away shrugged. "I didn't see a thing, Sheriff Gallon."

McCoy scowled. "What do you mean? You were right here and jumped out of the way. You were the first one to the body after he fell."

"Didn't see a thing, Sheriff."

Sheriff Gallon snorted and looked around. "Anybody else see what happened? Anybody who can say it was self-defense?"

No one said a word. McCoy still had the Colt in his hand.

"I'll have to ask you to come down to the jail, stranger. You're under arrest for murder."

McCoy lifted the Colt. "Better think again, Sheriff. You better ask your black robed leader about it first, don't you think? I hear there are some serious problems in the ranks, like one man got himself shot with a rifle last night. One of your own. You only

have twenty black robes now. More are falling by
the wayside. You can't cover up burning a man at
the stake very long."

"Don't know what you're talking about, stranger.
Heard you was a troublemaker."

"That what Halverson told you, was it?"

"Damn right. Hell, you can't get far. People all over
town will back me, not you."

"Don't be too sure." He turned to the crowd that
had gathered. "Aren't you people tired of being scared
to death by those black robed cowards? You saw
what they did to Shorty Clawson yesterday. They're
nothing but a bunch of yellow bellied cowards hiding
behind black robes. They are the criminals, not you
good folks. I'm here to help you put a stop to all of
this killing.

Now, who will testify that I shot Leonard in self-
defense?"

A woman stepped forward.

"I will. Leonard was a rat anyway. He shot at this
man and got himself hit in return. I saw the whole
thing."

"Yes, I saw it too," a man in his sixties said. "Damn
Leonard had a bad thing about guns. He used them too
much. I'll testify."

McCoy turned to the sheriff. "So, you still going to
put me in your jail?"

Chapter Twelve

Sheriff Gallon looked at the two witnesses, then over at McCoy. "You two are sure that it was self-defense, and you're willing to sign a statement to that effect?"

"Absolutely," the woman said.

The man nodded. "Way it happened, Sheriff."

Sheriff Gallon looked back at McCoy. "I reckon there ain't no reason to hold you then. Just see to it you don't get in no more trouble in Timber Break."

"When trouble comes looking for me, Sheriff, it's a mite hard to sidestep, especially when that trouble is packing a forty-five caliber six-gun."

The sheriff said nothing in reply, and McCoy went on down the street to the hardware store.

There were two customer's and McCoy waited until

both had bought merchandise and went out the front door.

"Mr. Oberholtzer, you passed out on me last night, do you remember? We were having a quiet little talk and you passed out, drunk as a skunk."

"Yeah, I do that from time to time. Yesterday was not a good day for me."

"Shorty Clawson was a friend of yours. I'm sorry. But it looks like you could have done something to save him." McCoy held up both hands when anger flared on Oberholtzer's face.

"I'm not criticizing you, just wondering. Of course I do have a way that you might be able to get back at the group."

"How, without them killing me?"

"Give me the name of the leader, the one behind this move to turn a little sex party into a murder machine."

"Hell, I told you last night that I wouldn't last twenty-four hours. I don't even know why they killed Thornton. Sheriff Gallon told everybody it was a robber who done it."

"Fred, I've got the solution to your problem. You tell me who the top two or three people are, then you catch the stage for Boise and stay for two weeks. By the time you come home, the town will be back to normal."

"Sure, and I won't have a job." Fred scowled. "Hell, I might not have a job, anyway." He picked up a box of lag screws and pushed it around the counter. "You know about the burning at the stake. Nobody said we would really fry the guy. It was all a bluff, a way to scare the old fellow into getting on the stage and never coming back."

"So who threw the torch on the kindling?" McCoy asked.

"That would be telling, and I'm not quite ready yet. Maybe in a day or so. I heard something is going on out at the mine. Any chance that they turned up a new vein of silver?"

"Always that chance."

"I used to work out there before the mine went dry. Maybe I could get a job again."

"Should pay more than running a store."

"Let me see what happens at the mine. Then you come back and see me tomorrow. I'll have an answer for you one way or the other."

McCoy shook the man's hand and went out the door. He suspected Lud Halverson. He had the motive. He had the most to lose in town if it got out Eloise Mae had been murdered here.

The only trouble was, McCoy had no proof. He had nothing to show to a county grand jury at a traveling circuit court judge. Evidence, eyewitnesses who would talk, proof that would hold up to a jury— that was what he needed.

He went toward the dress shop. Ever since the two had come forward and vouched for him as firing in self-defense, he had noticed a change in attitude among the people. They smiled more now. They held their heads up higher. They didn't look quickly away from him when he nodded at them.

Maybe things were changing all over town. He hoped so.

He stepped into the dress shop and saw that Mrs. Edwards had a customer. Jessica smiled and hurried up to him. She looked at the window, then reached up and kissed his lips and stepped back.

"That's the best way to say hello," she said softly.

"Hello yourself. I'm starting to get a handle on this problem. A couple of days it might be all wrapped up."

"Good, that's great news. Hey, have you had any lunch yet?"

He frowned. "No. I ate breakfast twice, but no lunch."

"You want to take me out to lunch? I can pay if you're short on cash."

"How brazen of you, Miss Edwards. I'm shocked and surprised. What would your aunt say?"

"It was her idea. She says a girl has to go after what she wants."

"Now that you mention it, I'm getting more hungry all the time."

"Aunt Wilda, I'm going out to lunch with Mr. McCoy. Be back in an hour or so."

"Yes, dear, that's fine."

They ate at the Old Growth Café, the other eatery in town. Both had two pieces of fried chicken, potato salad and iced tea. Jessie sat close to him in the small booth, and he could feel the pressure of her thigh against his.

"Can you come to the house tonight?" she asked him.

"Not sure. I might be in the middle of investigating something. I want to get this all tied up in a neat little bundle with the villains in jail or in their graves."

"You know about the burning at the stake and why they did it?"

"Yes. Not a pretty story."

"Tell me. I want to know what would make a whole town do this."

He told her about the woman who had come to town but didn't tell her she was the president's daughter. When he finished she nodded.

"So, you've got your killer. No doubt, it has to be Ludwig Halverson."

"Has to be, but I've got no proof, nothing to go to a judge or jury with. Until I get that, my hands are tied."

He felt her hand under the table resting on his leg.

"What can you do?" She looked at him, her eyes bright with the thrill of touching him in public even when no one could see. Her hand moved farther until it lay at his crotch. Slowly she rubbed his balls and his growing erection.

"I have to do something." He put his hand under the table and caught hers. "Something to take care of the situation."

Jessica pouted. "Maybe we could talk about it some more in the back room at the dress shop."

He lowered his voice. "I don't think so, Jess. Especially not on the cot."

She frowned, then took a deep breath. "You just want me to stay ignorant all my life about various things that are terribly important to me."

"True, the more ignorant the better wife you'll make. Looks like our lunch is about over." He moved her hand, slid out from the table and helped her out.

"That was a sneaky thing you just did," he said softly.

Jessica grinned. "A girl wants to find out things, that's all. Just some natural curiosity."

He paid the woman at the cash register, led Jessica outside and piloted her across the street to the door of the dress shop.

"Say thank you to the nice man for lunch," Spur prompted.

"Thank you sweet, sexy, nice man for lunch," she said softly and grinned.

McCoy chuckled. "You are something, aren't you? Now be good for a while and let me finish my work here. Then we'll have another little talk."

"Talk and touch?"

"We'll see." He turned and walked down the boardwalk. A rider came galloping into Main Street, the horse lathered and sweating. The rider stood up in his stirrups and screamed at the whole town.

"The Silver Strike Mine is reopening. New vein of silver ore found today. We're back in business!"

He rode down half a block and shouted the news again. In a few minutes it looked like half the town's citizens ran into Main Street. People were shouting and crying. Men had wide grins on their faces. It would mean good paying work for everyone.

The messenger came back shouting the news in more detail this time.

"Mrs. Barton says the mine will open just as soon as she can get it operating. Uriah Jordan will be hiring this afternoon in front of the Grubstake Saloon. He says he needs thirty men and three foremen not afraid of some manual labor to get the mine back in condition to start producing silver again. Regular operation should start in about a month. Then Mrs.

Barton says she'll put on two ten hour shifts."

A big cheer went up. A line started to form in front of the Grubstake Saloon, and McCoy leaned against the bank building and grinned. He wondered what this was going to do to Halverson's plans.

It also could change Fred Oberholtzer's plans. McCoy hurried down the boardwalk to the hardware store and went inside.

Oberholtzer sat on the small counter at the back working on a piece of paper. He saw McCoy and held out the paper.

"Here it is. With the mine opening again, I should be back at my old job as supervisor on the third level or wherever the hell the strike is. So I decided to do as you suggested. Here's a list of the twenty-one members of the Friday night club. That's what I called it. Everyone had his own name for the place.

"One of the women called it the Big Dong club. At least here's the list. The top man is my current boss, Ludwig Halverson. I'm willing to give you a signed statement to that effect and I'll be glad to testify in court, providing that Halverson is incarcerated at the time. Don't want him blowing my brains out like he did Thornton's."

McCoy took the list. The first name on it was Halverson's, followed by Leonard Diderman. He saw Thornton's name and several women's names and the last one, Fred Oberholtzer.

"Who were the leaders of the killings."

"The top two, Halverson and Leonard Diderman. Both of them had the most to lose. They were the ones who shot the woman who gave the men the syph. They got everyone else all worked up about protecting the town before we voted."

"What about Cheyenne? I see her name's on the list."

"A leader? No, she just ran the sexy parties. She didn't have nothing to do with the other part. Voted no on both of the killings. She told me so."

"That clears up one or two points." McCoy frowned. "You realize that there will have to be some kind of charges filed against the remaining nineteen of you for those two deaths. The evidence might be a little sparse. The judge could come up with a fine and probation, but I'm not promising anything."

"No, I figure I did an evil thing. Only right that I get punished for it, but I hope it ain't too severe."

McCoy folded the paper, then looked at it again and unfolded it.

"Fred, would you mind writing a note under those names, stating that these are the names of the individuals who participated in the burning of Colonel Amos Potter and the stoning of Shorty Clawson."

Fred took the pencil and wrote down what McCoy dictated.

"Now sign it. Then if I sign it as a witness, it should be about as legal as it can get."

"Should I close up and catch the stage?"

"Not yet. Nobody knows that you wrote this or that I have it. By the time Halverson finds out, I hope we have him in jail or ready for the undertaker. Keep your ears open. Any idea when the circuit court judge is due to get into town?"

"Not a one, Mr. McCoy. You might ask Vince Ihander, down about three doors. He's a lawyer of sorts, only one in town, so he might know."

Three stores down, McCoy opened the door to the lawyer's office. A thin, spry little man sat behind a desk reading a Chicago newspaper. He put his feet down and stared at McCoy through store-bought spectacles.

"Aye yep. Help you?"

"Mr. Ihander?"

"Tis truth."

"Do you know when the circuit court judge is due to be in town?"

"Aye yep. He was due three days ago, which should mean he could be here today or tomorrow."

"He come in by stage?"

"Not so. Has his own covered carriage. Fixed it up right nice so it's near a home to him. Got a bed in there and some cooking gear case he and his driver need to camp out overnight. Usually he's prompt. You need a lawyer?"

"No sir, but a batch of other folks in town damn well will. Does he stay at the hotel when he comes in?"

"Aye, yep. Only place in this little town for a stranger to bed down."

"That would be if you didn't count Hattie's place I would imagine."

The lawyer nodded. "Tis the truth, certainly tis."

McCoy thanked the little man and went back to the street. So now he had some evidence and some hard facts, but he couldn't trust the sheriff. He didn't even know if the county had a district attorney. He might come in on a circuit as well. Any grand jury would be appointed for specific cases by the circuit judge in all likelihood. McCoy wasn't sure how the Idaho

Territory was set up, but that was the system in many new territories.

He could set and wait and watch the reopening of the Silver Stake Mine. He could visit the marvelously sculptured and willing body of Cheyenne. He could go talk to the Edwards ladies and fight off pretty little Jessica. Maybe he should go and accuse Halverson of everything he knew about the situation, show him the identification card he carried and egg him into a fight so he could blow the bastard's brains out.

Without Halverson the whole group would fall apart. Maybe he didn't need the judge. This was one of those touchy situations where a brilliant attorney might get Halverson acquitted, or Halverson might simply buy the jury. Maybe a couple of .45 slugs would be the better way to go. He walked toward the Halverson building.

He was two doors away when he heard a commotion down the street. He watched as two teams of matched blacks came prancing down the middle of Main Street. Behind them was a fancy coach, painted black and orange with some light green trim. It had a door on the side with a gold handle. On a high seat on the rig's roof sat a black man in top hat and tails and a big grin as he maneuvered the carriage, missing as many manure piles as he could.

The horses all had black-stained leather harnesses and copper fittings and rings so it looked like a circus unit.

"The judge is here!" a small boy shouted as he raced out to the street to run alongside the high stepping blacks. Before the rig reached the hotel there were 30 boys and a few girls chasing it down the street.

A half hour later, Spur McCoy knocked on a hotel room door. A moment later the black man, minus the top hat but still in the black tie and tails, opened the door.

"I know the judge is tired and has had a long day, but I'm an out-of-state lawman with some serious legal problems that I need to see the judge about as soon as possible. I hope the judge has the time."

The black man nodded with great dignity. "I understand, suh. However, that is going to present some serious problems."

"Who is that at the door?" a brusk voice called from behind the black man.

"Gentleman who wants to see the judge," the black man said without turning around.

"This gent have a name?" the voice asked.

The black man looked up at Spur. "Suh?"

"Oh, yes, tell him my name is Spur McCoy."

A moment later the black man was pushed aside and a medium-sized man with a dark moustache and a scowling face and holding a sawed-off shotgun took his place. The weapon never wavered from where it centered on McCoy's chest.

"Come right in, McCoy," the man who held the shotgun said. "I been looking forward to this ever since I got the job this morning."

McCoy had no chance to dart out of range or to go for his weapon. He froze in place.

"Come on, come on, we're not formal here. Come in and meet the old judge and the new judge."

McCoy edged into the room, and the man kicked the door shut. McCoy stared in surprise at the man who sat in the chair, smoking a long brown cigar. It was Ludwig Halverson.

"McCoy, I was just telling the judge here about you. He agrees with me. We figure an accident will be best, with a complete report sent back to your office. The judge has some papers identifying you as a member of the United States Secret Service here on a special job for the president. I know all about why you're here, and why you're never going to leave Timber Break. We've decided that an accident would be best."

Halverson took a pull on the cigar and blew the smoke out at McCoy. "Judge Josiah H. Brandywine here agrees with me. Don't you judge?"

Halverson waved his cigar toward the far wall. McCoy saw a man sitting there tied to a chair with a gag in his mouth. His eyes stared hard at McCoy in a silent plea for help.

Chapter Thirteen

Spur McCoy looked back at Halverson who snorted. "Halverson, you are one stupid asshole, you know that? Kidnapping a circuit court judge. Wasn't killing the president's daughter enough for you? Now you're compounding your problems pulling a shotgun on me."

He looked at the man holding the sawed-off gun. "Hey, killer, you know that by the time you pull the trigger on that Remington, I'll have two .45 slugs in you. I might be dead and gone, but you'll be in hell right beside me. That what you want out of this? You could have a good job in the mine next month. You siding with this loser here, this asshole Halverson?"

"Don't listen to him," Halverson bellowed. "He's a dead man and he knows it, so he's talking big. No man can outdraw a trigger finger on the metal. He knows that."

The shotgunner glanced at his boss, then looked back at Spur. "You want me to kill him right now?"

"Not in front of a witness, stupid!" Halverson snarled.

When the shotgunner darted another look at his boss, McCoy made his move. His hand darted upward from where it had hung at his side and hit the butt of the Colt, pulling it out of leather. His finger probed into the trigger hole and his right thumb caught the hammer, pulling it backward before the muzzle cleared leather.

About the time the click of the cocking gun sounded, the shotgunner jerked his face back toward McCoy, and there was a split second of indecision whether to pull the trigger on the shotgun.

Then it didn't matter. McCoy's Colt fired, the explosion of the round in the small room sounding like hell with the sound booming as it bounced from wall to wall, deafening everyone in the room.

The round slanted slightly upward, drove through the shotgunner's left lung and rammed him three feet to the rear. He dropped the sawed off shotgun which went off when it hit the floor.

McCoy turned the .45 toward Halverson, but he wasn't there. He evidently had fled the second he saw Spur drawing his gun. The connecting door into the next hotel room was open.

McCoy darted that way, looked out the open ground floor window and caught a glimpse of Halverson sprinting out of the alley onto Main Street.

McCoy went back to the other room and checked the man who had held the shotgun. He was dead. He went to the judge in the chair and cut off the gag, then sliced away the strips of cloth that tied him to the chair.

"Young man, I thank you. That was quite an exhibition of the quick draw."

"Judge Brandywine?"

"I am now. Thought I was a dead man there for about half an hour. Glad you showed up, McCoy. I've been reading about you. Didn't know for sure why you were here, but I got a strongly worded message from the territorial governor to get my ass over here and see what was going on."

"A lot is going on, Judge. There's been a murder, and then more recently a man was burned at the stake, and yesterday another man was stoned to death. It's a little complicated, but I'll spell it out to you later. Right now, I'd suggest you arm yourself, not let anyone in the door and let me head out and try to find Halverson before he gets out of the territory."

"Yes, McCoy, you do that. No one will take us by surprise again. Washington, you heard what the man said. Go down to the carriage and bring up that brace of .45 pistols we have."

"Oh, don't rely on the local sheriff. He's part of the problem." McCoy opened the window, jumped through it to the ground and ran down to Main Street. There was no sign of the town's richest man. Where would he go? Probably to his office.

McCoy walked up to the office, stood by the outer wall and pushed open the door. No shots came through the opening.

He charged inside, his six-gun ready, but found only a crying Gwen.

"Don't need your gun. He's gone. Ran in here, grabbed the emergency satchel he keeps here in his safe and ran right on out the back of the building. He's probably halfway to the livery stable by now."

"What did he keep in the emergency bag?"

"Plenty of cash—his stocks and bonds and high denomination bank notes. He called it his getaway bag."

McCoy hurried outside and ran down the street, the Colt in his firm right hand and the leather holster slapping against his leg with every stride.

The stable man looked up and scowled. "Thought you was working for me," he said.

"Quit. Did Halverson just get out that bay and ride off?"

"No business of yours, but he did. Went north."

It took McCoy five minutes to get a horse, saddle it and ride off. He wasn't sure where Halverson was headed but all he could do was try to follow.

On the northern road ten minutes later, McCoy found a fresh set of tracks. The bay had been galloping, but she couldn't keep that up for long.

Five minutes later he found where the bay had slowed down to a walk. The road soon left the town and the last scattering of houses and kept to the side of the small river. There were rivers and creeks and streams all over this part of Idaho. They came from the heavy snow pack in the mountains in winter and the heavier rainfall during spring at the lower altitudes.

About two miles out of town, McCoy saw a glint of sunlight ahead as it bounced off metal or glass and bent low over his mount. A moment later a rifle cracked, and the round slammed through the air less than a foot over McCoy's shoulder.

McCoy slid off his mount, released her and dropped to the ground behind some rocks. Two rifle rounds ricocheted off the boulders as McCoy crouched below them. He had the bushwhacker spotted, about 50 yards ahead and across the trail.

A rifle against a six-gun was not good odds. McCoy watched the horse. She moved toward the side of the road and toward a fresh patch of green grass. If she kept going the same direction she would block the bushwhacker's line of fire.

He crouched, ready to move. The roan took three more steps and was directly blotting out the spot where the rifleman lay. McCoy sprinted the ten yards to the horse, turned her head and ran her across the road.

The rifleman realized too late that there were six legs under the horse instead of four, and he snapped a round at the animal, but missed her and McCoy as well. McCoy left the horse at the side of the trail and charged five yards into brush and trees in the edge of the small valley. He was out of sight of the bushwhacker.

Now, all he had to do was work forward quietly. He drew on his training with Indian friends and moved through the brush and trees toward the gunman with no more than the whisper of a brushed branch.

When he could see the top of the rocks the rifleman lay behind, he stopped. Was the man still there, or had he retreated? Why retreat when you outgun the other man? McCoy moved slower now, well-aware that the gunman could stand up at any time and see him plainly.

McCoy took two more steps, then eased himself down into the brush. He worked forward on his belly now, pushing with his toes and pulling with his elbows. Ten feet later he could see around the two boulders.

A man lay there, pushing new rounds into a Spencer ammunition tube. The range was 30 feet. McCoy sighted in on the shooter's right shoulder and squeezed off a shot. There were no branches or twigs in the way to throw off the lead. The round drove straight and true, blasting into the gunman's right shoulder and punching the Spencer rifle out of his hands. He flopped backward, screaming in pain.

McCoy moved up slowly, but when he leaned out from in back of a Douglas fir tree, he saw the man had no sidearm and was working feverishly with his left hand to try to stem the flow of blood from the hole in back of his right shoulder.

McCoy traversed the last ten feet without a sound and cocked his six-gun. The deadly sound of metal on metal jerked the man's head up and produced unbridled terror on his face.

"Don't kill me!"

"Why not?"

"Look, I'll tell you everything. All he told me. Halverson brought me along to slow you down. He's heading for a small hunting cabin about five miles on up this trail. Take a fork to the right near a lightning-shattered pine tree. Can't miss it."

"Hand me the Spencer, butt first."

The bearded man did as he was told.

"You want a service or just a six foot hole in the far end of the cemetery?"

Before the man could answer, McCoy shot him in the right arm. He rolled over on the ground, bellowing in pain.

"You shot me!"

"That's what you tried to do to me—with a rifle and from ambush. That can get you ten years in a federal prison. Where's your horse?"

"Over there in the brush a ways."

"Why didn't I see two sets of tracks coming up here?"

"Halverson told me to ride off the trail so you wouldn't be expecting two of us."

"Toss me your iron."

The man on the ground came to his knees and with his left hand took out his revolver and tossed it to McCoy, who caught it and pushed it in his belt.

"Now, on your feet. Go get your horse and ride back into town. Get that arm taken care of. Then ride south out of Timber Break. If I find you there when I get back, I'll kill you."

McCoy's level gaze and the deadly tone of his voice had a numbing effect on the bushwhacker who realized he could be dead instead of free and riding away. He nodded, hurried over to the brush, brought back his horse and rode off.

An old hunter's cabin? McCoy got his horse and rode north.

He found the turnoff, then rode slowly up the little used track. Half a mile from the main trail he saw a cabin with smoke coming from the chimney. Halverson was either stupid or supremely confident.

How could a bushwhacker miss with a Spencer rife at 20 feet?

The old log cabin had been there a long time. One side had fallen in, and there was no glass in one small window. The front door stood ajar, and one horse was at a hitching rail at the side. McCoy left his mount 50 yards away and moved up through heavy brush and timber. He heard nothing.

He came up on the blind side of the cabin and studied the layout. Nothing to do but charge in the front door. Maybe hit it with his shoulder and then dive inside with six-gun in hand.

He listened again. McCoy edged toward the door, his Colt cocked and ready. It could be another trap. Halverson had used enough of them. The lack of any sounds from inside bothered McCoy. Wouldn't the man be cooking something or humming or some damn thing?

He was three feet from the door now and could see part of the cabin's interior through the opening. It was dim inside. He could make out a chair and the edge of a fireplace. It was still too damned quiet.

McCoy crouched, ready to hit the door hard and blast it open with his shoulder.

He took a deep breath and charged. His shoulder jolted the door open on creaking hinges, then he dove inside the dimly lighted cabin.

No shotgun or revolver met him. He heard no cry of rage or surprise. There was only the creaking of the door and his own grunt as he landed on his right arm and shoulder, rolled and came to his knees, his Colt covering the cabin.

Six feet in front of McCoy, a man sat in a chair with his back to the door and didn't move. McCoy frowned, came to his feet and in three long strides moved around the side of the chair and stared at the man's face.

Halverson!

He sat there with his head down and his arms at his sides. Then Spur McCoy smelled the acid, slightly sweet smell of human blood. He looked at Halverson's hands and saw the twin pools of blood below red-stained fingers.

It took McCoy ten minutes to load Halverson's body on his horse and tie his hands and feet together under the horse's belly.

Timber Break would never be the same.

Chapter Fourteen

After Spur McCoy dropped off Lud Halverson's body at the undertaker, he had a long talk with Judge Brandywine. McCoy told the judge about the sequence of events from the first time Eloise Mae came to Timber Break and the trouble she caused there. He told the judge about the murder of Eloise Mae and the secret burial.

Then when a government man came around asking about the girl, Halverson and Leonard went crazy and decided there was only one way to keep the matter under cover. They set up the elaborate scheme to implicate half the town when Colonel Amos Potter had been burned at the stake.

McCoy had the list of the 21 conspirators. Of course, the list was reduced by three deaths.

At last they decided on the charges. All 18 of them, including the ten women, would be charged with manslaughter in two counts. McCoy wrote out separate charges for each one and signed them.

Judge Brandywine certified them and ordered all 18 to appear in his court the next day. Since they had no courthouse, the proceedings would be held in the Baptist church.

"I'd love to give them all a year in prison and five years probation," Judge Brandywine said. "But seeing these are first offenses, and the fact that they all were tricked into the first actual killing by the two ringleaders and then threatened and forced to help in the second, means that I'll go easy on them.

"I'm going to give them each five years probation. But if any of them get in trouble again, they'll have to answer for that, as well as serve five years for this one."

It was well past midnight when the judge and McCoy finished. McCoy walked down the street feeling relatively safe for the first time in days.

The judge would issue subpoenas the next day, and their hearing would be that afternoon at four o'clock. He figured that none would demand a trial. They would plead guilty and all would be sentenced that same day. The judge also issued an order stripping Sheriff Gallon of his authority and appointing one of his deputies as acting sheriff until a new one could be elected by county voters.

McCoy felt fine. It had been a strange case. He hadn't told the judge about Eloise Mae being the president's daughter. He had no need to know. McCoy expected he'd be summoned to the nation's capital to give the president a report in person. Such information simply could not be written down.

He turned the key in the lock on the back door of the dress store and slipped inside. The lamp was in its usual spot, and he lit it and carried it to where they had made up his bunk. He sat down on the cot, realizing how tired he was.

A moment later he turned when he heard a tittering laugh.

"Jessie, is that you?"

"No, I'm the ghost of your past loves come to haunt you." She stepped into the glow of the lamplight, and McCoy gasped in surprise.

She had put her red hair up on top of her head and wore a sleek black dress that outlined her body beautifully. Her cheeks had been touched up with hints of rouge, and her lips were reddened just a little.

Jessie hurried over and sat beside McCoy on the cot. "I know you might not be in town much longer," she said, her voice edged with tension and worry. "I didn't want to miss you. You aren't leaving town on the stage tomorrow, are you?"

"No, not tomorrow, but soon."

"The whole town knows about Halverson. He killed himself?"

McCoy nodded.

"Why did he go way up there in the woods to do it?"

"He might have decided after he got up there. There was no place to run."

"You even brought back his satchel that was loaded with money and stocks and bonds?"

"It wasn't mine. I left it at the bank. They will count it and record it for his heirs."

"I don't think he has any."

She moved closer to him. "Mr. McCoy, tonight I'm not going to let you get away from me. Aunt Wilda says a person must be positive and forceful. Oh, Charley has been over to the house two nights in a row now. I think he's sweet on Aunt Wilda. She said he was coming tonight, and she'd appreciate it if I could stay down here. You know, so I don't bother them tonight."

"Thoughtful of you."

"McCoy, don't be that way. You know what I'm getting at."

"Yes."

"Then we better do it. It's after midnight already."

Jessica sat there beside him, looking up. Her face was a mixture of desire and caution, of wanting and wondering.

"Wilda said I should tell you that it's kind of your responsibility to teach me everything. I mean you did start things—or we started things—and you got me all excited. She says it's better you show me in a soft gentle way than to have me jump some fourteen year-old and rape him." She looked at McCoy and laughed softly.

"Not that I would have to. Fourteen year-old boys have hard ones almost all the time. I've seen them at school." She leaned over, kissed McCoy on the lips and put her arms around him. She tried to push him down on the cot but he resisted.

Jessie took one of his hands and put it on her breast, then she rubbed the inside of his leg.

"Am I so ugly that you don't want to make love to me?"

"Of course not. You're beautiful, striking, sexy, a total delight. I don't want to spoil anything for you."

"Spoil it? You'll only make it better for me. I'll know what it's all about and I'll be able to protect myself if I get in a tough situation."

She kissed him again, and McCoy sighed.

"Oh, damn," he said. When his hand began to move on her breast, Jessie gave a small cry of delight and moved her hand from his leg up to his crotch where a swelling had taken place. He kissed her, his mouth open, tongue probing. She sighed and nodded and kissed him back.

Slowly they lay down on the cot. Her breasts pushed hard against his chest. She rolled a little so she was on top of him, her hips ginding against his.

"I like this," she said. "Gives me a feeling of importance, like I'm winning."

He unbuttoned her dress down the front and found her breasts naked underneath. He fondled them which brought a quick gasp of pleasure from Jessie.

She sat up and with great care lifted the dress over her head. She wore nothing under it. She then started taking his clothes off. First she removed his leather vest, then his shirt. She fondled his breasts and and stared wide-eyed at his hairy chest.

Jessie helped him off with his boots, his pants and his short underwear.

"Oh, how glorious! I've always wanted to undress a man. This is wild, just absolutely the most fun I've ever had."

McCoy grinned at her pleasure. She pulled his head down to her breasts.

"Please eat my titties. They love it so much. Just no words to describe how wonderful that makes me feel."

Jessie pushed him down on the cot and fell on top of him. Spasms ripped through her delightful young body, shaking her the way a big dog does with a small rabbit. She cried out in joy and then almost relaxed. As she looked down at him, another series of vibrations and shattering spasms tore into her, and she cried out louder this time, moaning and keening before they all passed and she gave one big sigh and dropped on top of him, exhausted.

He let her rest for a few minutes, then kissed the top of her head.

"Are you ready," he asked.

She looked at him closely, then smiled and nodded. Her hand went to his erection which she held tenderly.

"He's really big, you know that. Is there any way that he . . ."

McCoy chuckled. "Don't wonder about that. Remember from that same place is where a baby emerges. If you think about that you can see that there's going to be plenty of room. You'll see."

She shivered and hugged him. Slowly his hands moved down over her breasts to her legs. He turned her over so she lay on her back and her legs spread wide.

His hands worked down the inner side of her thighs, and he saw her muscles jerk in response. With one soft touch, his fingers brushed her heartland and she gasped.

"Oh, nice," she said. Her eyes were closed now, her arms at her sides.

His fingers touched her again, then gently massaged her soft, moist outer lips. He worked on them and felt more lubrication. In one quick stroke he pushed one finger deep inside her, and she humped her hips toward him and moaned in delight.

"Are you ready?" he asked.

"Oh, yes! I've been ready since the first day you kissed my titties. Right now, please, right now."

He leaned over her and gently touched her outer lips with his erection. She withdrew a moment, but then he felt her juices flowing. Gently he soaked in them a moment, then pushed forward.

After a moment of restriction, she relaxed, and he slid into her deeper and deeper. With each slow movement she gasped and shrilled in delight. When he was fully inserted, Jessica wailed in joy and fulfillment.

"Just wonderful!" she crooned. "So marvelous, so beautiful! I've never felt anything that was so fine and delightful. Oh, I could stay this way forever."

He stroked once, and her eyes went wide. He stroked again, and this time her hips came up to meet him. At the end of the stroke she ground her hips against him in a gentle circular motion.

He wondered how girls knew these things the first time. As he speeded up the poking, she moved faster with him. Her face was a soft glow of ecstasy.

"Wonderful . . . oh, wonderful . . . just wonderful!"

A few more strokes and he felt her building. She paced him, then surpassed him, her hips crashing, her body writhing. Hot breath billowed from her mouth, and she roared in primitive delight as she raced into another climax.

Twice he thought she was finished, then she jolted into another long series of spasms as she climaxed again.

At last she whimpered and lay still.

A moment later her eyes snapped open. "I did, but you didn't yet."

He slammed into her five times then felt the fluids pouring through his tubes and finished his own climax.

They lay there panting.

"Now the next time, I think we should . . ."

He shook his head and held up his hand, stopping her.

"No. That was probably the best you'll ever have. Dream about that one until you get married. Anything else now would not be as good and might leave you wondering. Hold onto that one, it was fine and good. Remember it."

He reached for his drawers and put them on, then took the two blankets at the foot of the cot and spread them out on the floor.

"You, young lady, are going to go to sleep. I'm going to sleep here on the floor. We'll be up early for breakfast."

Her lips turned into a pout.

McCoy laughed, reached down and kissed her. "Hey, I didn't say this was going to be an all-night orgy. That comes much later. Right now, just remember and think about it and go to sleep if you can. You'll make some lucky man a wonderful, sexy wife."

"But not you, Spur McCoy?"

"Not me. I'm not the marrying kind. At least not right now. So settle down. Tomorrow isn't too far away."

He pushed his pants under the blankets for his pillow, turned over and went to sleep.

Jessie didn't sleep for more than an hour, and when sleep did come, she had a wonderful smile of remembrance on her pretty face.

Early the next morning, just after six, Spur McCoy was up, dressed and kneeling down beside the cot. He reached over and kissed her on the cheek. She smiled and turned toward him. He kissed her lips, and she moaned. Then her eyes came open and she smiled.

"Hi, marvelous man."

"Hi, yourself, wonderful lady."

When she sat up, the sheet fell away showing her firm young breasts, but she gave no hint of embarrassment. "I don't suppose that you would consider . . ."

He cut her off. "Not in a year and a half. What I will consider is you getting dressed so we can go out to breakfast. We wouldn't want to disturb your aunt."

Jessie grinned. "I wonder if Charlie stayed all night?"

"You and Wilda can compare notes later. Let's get some breakfast."

Later that morning the subpoenas were delivered and served. All the people were instructed to report to the Baptist church that afternoon at four o'clock for a hearing.

Everyone showed up. Judge Brandywine read them a long list of offenses and challenged them to defend themselves. No one had anything to say in defense of the charges.

"Now, since none of you have any defense, I want to hear how you plead to the charges. I'll read off the names one at a time, and you respond." He did. All 18 pleaded guilty.

After a serious scolding, the judge sentenced them. Each had pled guilty to manslaughter on two counts, but because of mitigating circumstances they were all sentenced to five years in prison, suspended, and each put on probation for the five years.

"Your honor, isn't this a bit unusual? We didn't have no trial or anything?" The question was asked by Harley Fritson, a carpenter by trade and a bachelor.

"That's true. You plead guilty. If you want a trial I'll allow you to plead not guilty. Then I'll arrange a trial for you here in three months. Until that time you're to remain in jail. I'll guarantee that you'll get at least ten years in prison if you face a jury of your peers."

"Oh," Fritson said, "forget I said a word, Judge."

Cheyenne Barton caught up with Spur as they left the church. She stared at him and shook her head.

"All the time you were a lawman and I didn't know it. Damn! Usually I can sniff out a lawman at twenty paces." She lifted her brows. "Well, forget that. You have time to come to my house for a celebration supper? Celebrating the opening of the mine, of course. I'll have eighty men working within two months. Need to bring in more workmen. This town will boom again.

"I owe it all to you. I was about ready to sell Halverson the mine. I was sure it was worked out.

I would have been giving away at least five million dollars. I owe it all to you. May I give you a going away present of a hundred thousand dollars?"

"I'm a federal law officer, Cheyenne. I can't accept a gift or gratuity of any kind."

"Then let's not think monetary. How about that dinner, and then me and you in my big bed all night?"

Spur chuckled. It had been a long time since he'd seen a body like Cheyenne's. It would be a long time again.

"Just might be able to make the time. First I want to check with the new sheriff, and then give my thanks to a few people. Would six this evening be a good time?"

Cheyenne smiled and caught his arm. She pulled him against her side, and his arm rubbed her breast. "I'd say six o'clock will be a fine time. Get there early if you can."

He left her and hurried down the street. A talk with the new sheriff, then a few words with Wilda and Jessie, and his work here would be done. He couldn't send a telegram until he got to Boise. Then he'd report what he could. Colonel Amos Potter had been murdered and buried in Timber Break, Idaho Territory. His killer had been caught and died at his own hand. The local situation was resolved and life was back to normal in Timber Break. He'd tell the rest of the story to the president when asked to do so.

McCoy's mind jumped ahead as if he were playing a tough chess game. He'd leave by stage in the morning and get to Boise where he could send a telegram to his boss in Washington D.C. the same day. He'd wait there two days for any reply and then start wondering

about what his next assignment might be. What would
it be, and where would his job as a Secret Service
Agent take him next? Spur McCoy grinned. He had
the best job in the whole world!

GIANT
SPECIAL EDITION

SPUR

DIRK FLETCHER

In these Special Giant Editions, Secret Service Agent Spur McCoy comes up against more bullets and beauties than even he can handle.

Klondike Cutie. A boomtown full of the most ornery vermin ever to pan a river, Dawson is the perfect place for a killer to hide—until Spur McCoy arrives. Fresh from a steamboat and the steamiest woman he's ever staked a claim on, McCoy knows the chances of mining gold are very good in the Klondike. And to his delight, the prospects for golden gals are even better.
_3420-4 $4.99 US/$5.99 CAN

High Plains Princess. Riding herd over a princess touring the Wild West isn't the easiest assignment Spur has ever had, especially since assassins are determined to end young Alexandria's reign. But before the last blow is dealt, Spur will shoot his pistol aplently and earn himself a knighthood for seeing to the monarch's special needs.
_3260-0 $4.50 US/$5.50 CAN

LEISURE BOOKS
ATTN: Order Department
276 5th Avenue, New York, NY 10001

Please add $1.50 for shipping and handling for the first book and $.35 for each book thereafter. PA., N.Y.S. and N.Y.C. residents, please add appropriate sales tax. No cash, stamps, or C.O.D.s. All orders shipped within 6 weeks via postal service book rate. Canadian orders require $2.00 extra postage and must be paid in U.S. dollars through a U.S. banking facility.

Name _____

Address _____

City _____ State _____ Zip _____

I have enclosed $_____in payment for the checked book(s).
Payment <u>must</u> accompany all orders.☐ Please send a free catalog.

GIANT SPECIAL EDITION

BUCKSKIN
SIX-GUN SHOOTOUT
—— KIT DALTON ——

More girls...more guns...
more rip-roarin' adventure!

Only a man with a taste for hot lead and a hankering for fancy ladies can survive in the Old West—a man like Buckskin Lee Morgan. And when an old girlfriend calls on Morgan to find the gutless murderer who ambushed her husband, he is more than ready to act as judge, jury, and executioner. For Morgan lives by one law: anyone who messes with his women is a dead man!

_3383-6 $4.50 US/$5.50 CAN

KANSAN DOUBLE EDITIONS
By Robert E. Mills

*A double shot of hard lovin' and straight shootin'
in the Old West for one low price!*

Showdown at Hells Canyon. Sworn to kill his father's murderer, young Davy Watson rides a vengeance trail that leads him from frontier ballrooms and brothels to the wild Idaho territory.
And in the same action-packed volume...
Across the High Sierra. Recovering from a brutal gun battle, the Kansan is tended to by three angels of mercy. But when the hot-blooded beauties are kidnapped, he has to ride to hell and back to save his own slice of heaven.
__3342-9 $4.50

Red Apache Sun. When his sidekick Soaring Hawk helps two blood brothers break out of an Arizona hoosegow, Davy Watson finds a gun in his back—and a noose around his neck!
And in the same rip-roarin' volume...
Judge Colt. In the lawless New Mexico Territory, the Kansan gets caught between a Mexican spitfire and an American doxy fighting on opposite sides of a range war.
__3373-9 $4.50